Illusion Two
fables, fantasies and metafictions

Illusion Two

FABLES, FANTASIES AND METAFICTIONS

- EDITED BY -

GEOFF HANCOCK

Aya Press, 1983

CANADIAN CATALOGUING IN PUBLICATION DATA

Main entry under title:
Illusion: fables, fantasies and metafictions

ISBN 0-920544-27-4 (v. 1). — ISBN 0-920544-28-2 (v. 2).
ISBN 0-920544-29-0 (set).

1. Short stories, Canadian (English).* I. Hancock, Geoff, 1946-

V. 2   .PS8329.I44   C813'.0108   C83-094157-6
PR9197.32.I44

50,019

Cover © Virgil Burnett, 1983.

Shoeless Joe Jackson Comes to Iowa is reprinted from the book of the same name by permission of Oberon Press. *The Veteran* originally appeared in *One Cook, Once Dreaming* (Sono Nis). Some of these stories originally appeared in *Canadian Fiction Magazine, The Malahat Review, Exile,* and *TriQuarterly. Unless the Eye Catch Fire* appeared in *Evening Dance of the Grey Flies* published by Oxford University Press and is reprinted by permission.

Illusion Two, edited by Geoff Hancock, is published February 1983 by Glynn Davies under the imprint of Aya Press in an edition of 1000 copies. Designed by Glynn Davies with Tim Inkster. Typeset in Palatino by Howarth & Smith Limited (Toronto) and executed by The Porcupine's Quill, Inc. (Erin).

ISBN 0-920544-27-4 (v. 1)
       0-920544-28-2 (v. 2)
       0-920544-29-0 (set)

Contents

Preface

Geoff Hancock

The weather: blizzard. Time: midnight. Place: my study. One Saturday night, in February 1981, I threw my typewriter, manuscript still in the carriage, across the room and out the window. Wheels, gears, the alphabet, popped and flew all over. Reason: Canadian Literature carries within itself elements of its own destruction. Realism, which became a force in the world's fiction as the Industrial Revolution generated the dynamic forces of machinery and technology, has now reached the end of its conveyor belt. As the push and pull of the assembly line declines, so does realistic fiction. The writers in *Illusion* are part of a second Romantic Rebellion in human artistic nature. They write not of what is in front of them, but of the marvellous that lies within, tempered with elements of our contemporary anguish.

'. . . all the maps you have are of no use, all this work of discovery and surveying; you have to start off at random, like the first man on earth; you risk dying of hunger a few miles from the richest stores . . .'

Michel Butor, *Degrees*

'She took one or two of them down and turned the pages over, trying to persuade herself she was reading them. But the meaning of words seemed to dart away from her like a shoal of minnows as she advanced upon them, and she felt more uneasy still.'

Michel Frayn, *Against Entropy*

'I saw all the mirrors in the planet, and none reflected me.'

Jorge Luis Borges

'Red is the most joyful and most dreadful thing in the physical universe; it is the fiercest note, it is the highest light, it is the place where the walls of this world of ours wear the thinnest and something beyond burns through.'

G.K. Chesterton

'How can anyone believe that a given work of art is an *object* independent of the psyche and personal history of the critic studying it, with regards to which he enjoys a sort of extraterritorial status?'

Roland Barthes, *Criticism as Language*

'Modern Art, like modern science, can establish complimentary relations with discredited fictional systems; as Newtonian mechanics is to quantum mechanics, so *King Lear* is to *Endgame*.'

Frank Kermode, *The Sense of Ending*

'Materialism. Utter the word with horror, stressing each syllable.'

Gustave Flaubert, *The Dictionary of Accepted Ideas*

Illusion Two raises the possibility that a fiction of the marvellous will be a major force in Canadian short stories. As French Literature in the 1880s turned into a new century, its revolving door was given that extra push by Apollinaire and others. So Canadian Literature is being pushed. Time is its own fiction, and out of the ruins of our contemporary landscape a new fiction is forming. Art works out of the inexplicable, and it is too dangerous to stand still as the revolving door of fiction swirls past. But the new fiction has a way of illuminating the old. These fables, fantasies, and metafictions finally reveal our true selves.

Fables, fantasies, and metafictions are a return to story telling. We reach the future, so the Mayan gods note in their chronicles, by travelling backwards. Canadian Literature has had a phenomenal growth in the past two decades. But it also has had its disappointments. Its shortcomings open the way for new possibilities. *Illusion* does not contain mirror-like stories, and indeed, the mirror is itself the symbol of the illusion. These stories are the memory traces of a forgotten reality now arriving at the forefront of Canadian short fiction. The writers in *Illusion* I and II travelled at random, they risked getting lost, but they returned with a broader conception of realism and fictional experience.

These stories do not depend on a narrow allegiance to the often limited demands of Canadian Literature. The past decades have been our own prehistory. Too much of our literary potential has been confined by less inventive narrative techniques.

The stories in *Illusion* are written by Canadian writers from coast to coast. This group, who plugged independently into similar energies, opens up the wider subsystem of the Canadian fictional experience. The crust of our frozen fictions is melting off, allowing great spouts of lava to spurt from long fissures. Illusions are known, yet unknown, until they are (re)discovered. Critics might leap upon definitions, try to limit the possibilities. But when writers work from artistic intuition, their karma will run over professional dogma.

The images in *Illusion* contain common elements transformed. In the stage sets of our daily activities, we find, as James Ross notes in 'Mythical Beasts', the rarely studied mythologies. And mythology, after all, is a system of metaphors which illuminates our lives as these stories do. Paradoxically, the fiction writers emphasize the *fiction* in their stories, as artfully created narrative constructions. They turn their backs, as Julio Cortazar has said, on what we might consider normal. In the fables and fantasies of *Illusion*, certainty is found in the visionary dream, as in Jane Urquhart's 'Five Wheelchairs', or the dreams of David Sharpe's narrator in 'Niagara Fall'. We find deep psychological fear in the folk tales of Virgil Burnett's 'Queen Constance' or Howard O'Hagan's 'Ursus' or Derk Wynand's 'The Veteran'. The alienated or paranoid state of mind is found in 'The Hot House' by Claudette Charbonneau-Tissot or 'Haunt' by Sean Virgo. In the metafictions, we find the fantastic, the ironical, and the intellectual resourcefulness of the fiction writer mingled with absurd and sometimes pessimistic views of the despairs of contemporary life. The extraordinary, such as the witch-goddess in McKevitt's 'The Steps', suddenly interrupts the mundane. Innovation is found in a rapidly shifting point of view, as in the gangster's threatening phone calls in George Bowering's 'Arbre de Décision'. Or perhaps the innovation may be in the form of an alien or grotesque character, such as flame-spirit of George McWhirter's 'Quarantine'. The writers in *Illusion* use all the technical resources they have to build and control that slender bridge between the unconscious and the conscious.

Both *Illusion* I and II will recall Sir Alfred Maury's 'hypnogogic images', and in this existence of wakeful dreaming, fiction moves closer to poetry, bending form to vision. *Illusion* is in that place where language discovers and discloses. In fiction, the writer releases the real image, the imagined image, the recon-

9

structed image, the collage image. These are not stories that limit, define, delineate, or border meanings. The forces of imaginative fiction, unleashed, cannot be held down to a single meaning. In the endless sentence that is the wonder of fiction, each of these stories is a single adjective, modifying the unnamed noun that is the future of Canadian fiction.

Why do writers turn to the marvellous? Fables, fantasies, and metafictions are stories of the alienated writer. The writer who wants to break away. Somewhere in each of these stories is the anguish of writers unsatisfied with their contemporary homeland, and the structures that have bound them to *place*. These stories direct us, not to where we live, but to how we live, not to where we've been, but to where we might go.

Shoeless Joe Jackson
Comes to Iowa

W. P. Kinsella

MY FATHER SAID he saw him years later playing in a tenth-rate commercial league in a textile town in Carolina, wearing shoes and an assumed name.

'He'd put on 50 pounds and the spring was gone from his step in the outfield, but he could still hit. Oh, how that man could hit. No-one has ever been able to hit like Shoeless Joe.'

Two years ago at dusk on a spring evening, when the sky was a robin's-egg blue and the wind as soft as a day-old chick, as I was sitting on the verandah of my farm home in eastern Iowa, a voice very clearly said to me, 'If you build it, he will come.'

The voice was that of a ballpark announcer. As he spoke, I instantly envisioned the finished product I knew I was being asked to conceive. I could see the dark, squarish speakers, like ancient sailors' hats, attached to aluminum-painted light standards that glowed down into a baseball field, my present position being directly behind home plate.

In reality, all anyone else could see out there in front of me was a tattered lawn of mostly dandelions and quack grass that petered out at the edge of a cornfield perhaps 50 yards from the house.

Anyone else was my wife Annie, my daughter Karin, a corn-coloured collie named Carmeletia Pope, and a cinnamon and white guinea pig named Junior who ate spaghetti and sang each time the fridge door opened. Karin and the dog were not quite two years old.

'If you build it, he will come,' the announcer repeated in scratchy Middle American, as if his voice had been recorded on an old 78-rpm record.

A three-hour lecture or a 500-page guide book could not have given me clearer directions: dimensions of ballparks jumped over and around me like fleas, cost figures for light standards and floodlights whirled around my head like the moths that dusted against the porch light above me.

That was all the instruction I ever received: two announcements and a vision of a baseball field. I sat on the verandah until the satiny dark was complete. A few curdly clouds striped the moon and it became so silent I could hear my eyes blink.

Our house is one of those massive old farm homes, square as a biscuit box with a sagging verandah on three sides. The floor of the verandah slopes so that marbles, baseballs, tennis balls and ball bearings all accumulate in a corner like a herd of cattle clustered with their backs to a storm. On the north verandah is a wooden porch swing where Annie and I sit on humid August nights, sip lemonade from teary glasses, and dream.

When I finally went to bed, and after Annie inched into my arms in that way she has, like a cat that you suddenly find sound asleep in your lap, I told her about the voice and I told her that I knew what it wanted me to do.

'Oh love,' she said, 'if it makes you happy you should do it,' and she found my lips with hers, and I shivered involuntarily as her tongue touched mine.

Annie: she has never once called me crazy. Just before I started the first landscape work, as I stood looking out at the lawn and the cornfield wondering how it could look so different in daylight, considering the notion of accepting it all as a dream and abandoning it, Annie appeared at my side and her arm circled my waist. She leaned against me and looked up, cocking her head like one of the red squirrels that scamper along the power lines from the highway to the house, 'Do it, love,' she said, as I looked down at her, that slip of a girl with hair the colour of cayenne pepper and at least a million freckles on her face and arms, that girl who lives in blue jeans and T-shirts and at 24 could still pass for sixteen.

I thought back to when I first knew her. I came to Iowa to study. She was the child of my landlady. I heard her one afternoon outside my window as she told her girlfriends, 'When I grow up I'm going to marry . . .' and she named me. The others were going to be nurses, teachers, pilots or movie stars, but Annie chose me as her occupation. She was ten. Eight years later we were married. I chose willingly, lovingly to stay in Iowa, eventually rented this farm, bought this farm, operating it one inch from bankruptcy. I don't seem meant to farm, but I want to be close to this precious land, for Annie and me to be able to say, 'This is ours.'

Now I stand ready to cut into the cornfield, to chisel away a piece of our livelihood to use as dream currency, and Annie says, 'Oh, love, if it makes you happy you should do it.' I carry her words in the back of my mind, stored the way a maiden aunt might wrap a brooch, a remembrance of a long-lost love. I understand how hard that was for her to say and how it got harder as the project advanced. How she must have told her family not to ask me about the baseball field I was building, because they stared at me dumb-eyed, a row of silent, thick-set peasants with red faces. Not an imagination among them except to forecast the wrath of God that will fall on the heads of pagans such as I.

He, of course, was Shoeless Joe Jackson.

Joseph Jefferson (Shoeless Joe) Jackson
Born: Brandon Mills, s.c., 16 July, 1887
Died: Grenville, s.c., 5 December, 1951

In April, 1945, Ty Cobb picked Shoeless Joe as the best left fielder of all time.

He never learned to read or write. He created legends with a bat and a glove. He wrote records with base hits, his pen a bat, his book History.

Was it really a voice I heard? Or was it perhaps something inside me making a statement that I did not hear with my ears but with my heart? Why should I want to follow this command? But as I ask, I already know the answer. I count the loves in my life: Annie, Karin, Iowa, Baseball. The great god Baseball.

My birthstone is a diamond. When asked, I say my astrological sign is 'hit and run' which draws a lot of blank stares here in Iowa where 30,000 people go to see the University of Iowa Hawkeyes football team while 30 regulars, including me, watch the baseball team perform.

My father, I've been told, talked baseball statistics to my mother's belly while waiting for me to be born.

My father: born, Glen Ullin, N.D., 14 April, 1896. Another diamond birthstone. Never saw a professional baseball game until 1919 when he came back from World War I where he was gassed at Passchendaele. He settled in Chicago where he inhabited a room above a bar across from Comiskey Park and quickly learned to live and die with the White Sox. Died a little when, as prohibitive favourites, they lost the 1919 World Series to Cincinnati, died a lot the next summer when eight members of the team were accused of throwing that World Series.

Before I knew what baseball was, I knew of Connie Mack, John McGraw, Grover Cleveland Alexander, Ty Cobb, Babe Ruth, Tris Speaker, Tinker-to-Evers-to-Chance, and, of course, Shoeless Joe Jackson. My father loved under-dogs, cheered for

13

the Brooklyn Dodgers and the hapless St. Louis Browns, loathed the Yankees, which I believe was an inherited trait, and insisted that Shoeless Joe was innocent, a victim of big business and crooked gamblers.

That first night, immediately after the voice and the vision, I did nothing except sip my lemonade a little faster and rattle the ice cubes in my glass. The vision of the baseball park lingered — swimming, swaying — seeming to be made of red steam, though perhaps it was only the sunset. There was a vision within the vision: one of Shoeless Joe Jackson playing left field. Shoeless Joe Jackson who last played major league baseball in 1920 and was suspended for life, along with seven of his compatriots, by Commissioner Keneshaw Mountain Landis, for his part in throwing the 1919 World Series.

'He hit .375 against the Reds in the 1919 World Series and played errorless ball,' my father would say, scratching his head in wonder.

Instead of nursery rhymes, I was raised on the story of the Black Sox Scandal, and instead of Tom Thumb or Rumpelstiltskin, I grew up hearing of the eight disgraced ballplayers: Weaver, Cicotte, Risberg, Felsch, Gandil, Williams, McMullin, and always, Shoeless Joe Jackson.

'Twelve hits in an eight-game series. And *they* suspended *him*,' father would cry, and Shoeless Joe became a symbol of the tyranny of the powerful over the powerless. The name Keneshaw Mountain Landis became synonymous with the Devil.

It is more work than you might imagine to build a baseball field. I laid out a whole field, but it was there in spirit only. It was really only left field that concerned me. Home plate was made from pieces of cracked two-by-four imbedded in the earth. The pitcher's mound rocked like a cradle when I stood on it. The bases were stray blocks of wood, unanchored. There was no backstop or grandstand, only one shaky bleacher beyond the left field wall. There was a left field wall, but only about 50 feet of it, twelve feet high, stained dark green and braced from the rear. And the left field grass. My intuition told me that it was the grass that was important. It took me three seasons to hone that grass to its proper texture, to its proper colour. I made trips to Minneapolis and one or two other cities where the stadiums still have natural grass infields and outfields. I would arrive hours before a game and watch the groundskeepers groom the field like a prize animal, then stay after the game when in the cool of the night the same groundsmen appeared with hoses, hoes, rakes, and patched the grasses like medics attending wounded soldiers.

I pretended to be building a little league ballfield and asked their secrets and sometimes was told. I took interest in their total operation; they wouldn't understand if I told them I was building only a left field.

Three seasons I've spent seeding, watering, fussing, praying, coddling that field like a sick child until it glows parrot-green, cool as mint, soft as moss, lying there like a cashmere blanket. I began watching it in the evenings, sitting on the rickety bleacher just beyond the fence. A bleacher I had constructed for an audience of one.

My father played some baseball, Class B teams in Florida and California. I found his statistics in a dusty minor league record book. In Florida, he played for a team called the Angels and, by his records, was a better-than-average catcher. He claimed to have visited all 48 states and every major-league ballpark before, at 40, he married and settled down a two-day drive from the nearest major league team. I tried to play, but ground balls bounced off my chest and fly balls dropped between my hands. I might have been a fair designated hitter, but the rule was too late in coming.

There is the story of the urchin who, tugging at Shoeless Joe Jackson's sleeve as he emerged from a Chicago courthouse, said, 'Say it ain't so, Joe.'

Jackson's reply reportedly was, 'I'm afraid it is, kid.'

When he comes, I won't put him on the spot by asking. The less said the better. It is likely that he did accept some money from gamblers. But throw the Series? Never! Shoeless Joe led both teams in hitting in that 1919 Series. It was the circumstances. The circumstances. The players were paid peasant salaries while the owners became rich. The infamous Ten Day Clause, which voided contracts, could end any player's career without compensation, pension, or even a ticket home.

The second spring, on a tooth-achy May evening, a covering of black clouds lumbered off westward like ghosts of buffalo and the sky became the cold colour of a silver coin. The forecast was for frost.

The left-field grass was like green angora, soft as a baby's cheek. In my mind I could see it dull and crisp, bleached by frost, and my chest tightened.

Then I used a trick a groundskeeper in Minneapolis taught me, saying it was taught to him by grape farmers in California. I

15

carried out a hose and making the spray so fine it was scarcely more than fog, I sprayed the soft, shaggy, spring grass all that chilled night. My hands ached and my own face became wet and cold, but as I watched, the spray froze on the grass, enclosing each blade in a gossamer-crystal coating of ice. A covering that served like a coat of armour to dispel the real frost that was set like a weasel upon killing in the night. I seemed to stand taller than ever before as the sun rose, turning the ice to eye-dazzling droplets, each a prism, making the field an orgy of rainbows.

Annie and Karin were at breakfast when I came in, the bacon and coffee smells and their laughter pulling me like a magnet.

'Did it work, love?' Annie asked, and I knew she knew by the look on my face that it did. And Karin, clapping her hands and complaining of how cold my face was when she kissed me, loved every second of it.

'And how did he get a name like Shoeless Joe?' I would ask my father, knowing full well the story but wanting to hear it again. And no matter how many times I heard it, I would still picture a lithe ballplayer, his great bare feet, white as baseballs, sinking into the outfield grass as he sprinted for a line drive. Then, after the catch, his toes gripping the grass like claws, he would brace and throw to the infield.

'It wasn't the least bit romantic,' my dad would say. 'When he was still in the minor leagues he bought a new pair of spikes and they hurt his feet; about the sixth inning he took them off and played the outfield in just his socks. The other players kidded him, called him Shoeless Joe, and the name stuck for all time.'

It was hard for me to imagine that a sore-footed young outfielder taking off his shoes one afternoon not long after the turn of the century could generate a legend.

I came to Iowa to study, one of the thousands of faceless students who pass through large universities, but I fell in love with Iowa. Fell in love with the land, the people, with the sky, the cornfields and Annie. Couldn't find work in my field, took what I could get. For years, each morning I bathed and frosted my cheeks with Aqua Velva, donned a three-piece suit and snap-brim hat, and, feeling like Superman emerging from a telephone booth, set forth to save the world from a lack of life insurance. I loathed the job so much that I did it quickly, urgently, almost violently. It was Annie who got me to rent the farm. It was Annie who got me to buy it. I operate it the way a child fits together his first puzzle, awkwardly, slowly, but when a piece slips into the proper slot, with pride and relief and joy. I built the field and waited, and waited, and waited. 'It will happen, honey,' Annie would say when I stood shaking my head at my folly. People look at me. I must have a nickname in town. But I could feel the magic building like a storm gathering. It felt as if small animals were scurrying through my veins. I knew it was going to happen soon.

'There's someone on your lawn,' Annie says to me, staring out into the orange-tinted dusk. 'I can't see him clearly, but I can tell someone is there.' She was quite right, at least about it being *my* lawn, although, it is not in the strictest sense of the word a lawn, it is a *left field*.

I watch Annie looking out. She is soft as a butterfly, Annie is, with an evil grin and a tongue that travels at the speed of light. Her jeans are painted to her body and her pointy little nipples poke at the front of a black T-shirt with the single word RAH! emblazoned in waspish yellow capitals. Her red hair is short and curly. She has the green eyes of a cat.

Annie understands, though it is me she understands, and not always what is happening. She attends ballgames with me and squeezes my arm when there's a hit, but her heart isn't in it and she would just as soon be at home. She loses interest if the score isn't close or the weather warm, or the pace fast enough. To me it is baseball and that is all that matters. It is the game that is important — the tension, the strategy, the ballet of the fielders, the angle of the bat.

I have been more restless than usual this night. I have sensed the magic drawing closer, hovering somewhere out in the night like a zeppelin, silky and silent, floating like the moon until the time is right.

Annie peeks through the drapes. 'There *is* a man out there; I can see his silhouette. He's wearing a baseball uniform, an old-fashioned one.'

'It's Shoeless Joe Jackson,' I say. My heart sounds like someone flicking a balloon with their index finger.

'Oh,' she says. Annie stays very calm in emergencies. She Band-aids bleeding fingers and toes, and patches the plumbing with gum and good wishes. Staying calm makes her able to live with me. The French have the right words for Annie — she has a good heart.

'Is he the Jackson on TV? The one you yell, "Drop it, Jackson," at?'

Annie's sense of baseball history is not highly developed.
'No, that's Reggie. This is Shoeless Joe Jackson. He hasn't played major league baseball since 1920.'
'Well, aren't you going to go out and chase him off your lawn, or something?'
Yes. What am I going to do? I wish someone else understood. My daughter has an evil grin and bewitching eyes. She climbs into my lap and watches television baseball with me. There is a magic about her.
'I think I'll go upstairs and read for a while,' Annie says. 'Why don't you invite Shoeless Jack in for coffee?' I feel the great tenderness toward her then, something akin to the rush of love I felt the first time I held my daughter in my arms. Annie senses that magic is about to happen. She knows that she is not part of it. My impulse is to pull her to me as she walks by, the denim of her thighs making a tiny music. But I don't. She will be waiting for me and she will twine her body about me and find my mouth with hers.

As I step out on the verandah, I can hear the steady drone of the crowd, like bees humming on a white afternoon, and the voices of the vendors, like crows cawing.

A little ground mist, like wisps of gauze, snakes in slow circular motions just above the grass.

'The grass is soft as a child's breath,' I say to the moonlight. On the porch wall I find the switch, and the single battery of floodlights I have erected behind the left-field fence sputters to life. 'I've shaved it like a golf green, tended it like I would my own baby. It has been powdered and lotioned and loved. It is ready.'

Moonlight butters the whole Iowa night. Clover and corn smells are thick as syrup. I experience a tingling like the tiniest of electric wires touching the back of my neck, sending warm sensations through me like the feeling of love. Then, as the lights flare, a scar against the blue-black sky, I see Shoeless Joe Jackson standing out in left field. His feet spread wide, body bent forward from the waist, hands on hips, he waits. There is the sharp crack of the bat and Shoeless Joe drifts effortlessly a few steps to his left, raises his right hand to signal for the ball, camps under it for a second or two, catches the ball, at the same time transferring it to his throwing hand, and fires it into the infield.

I make my way to left field, walking in the darkness far outside the third-base line, behind where the third-base stands would be. I climb up on the wobbly bleacher behind the fence. I can look right down on Shoeless Joe. He fields a single on one hop and pegs the ball to third.

'How does it play?' I holler down.

'The ball bounces true,' he replies.

'I know.' I am smiling with pride and my heart thumps mightily against my ribs. 'I've hit a thousand line drives and as many grounders. It's true as a felt-top table.'

'It is,' says Shoeless Joe. 'It is true.'

I lean back and watch the game. From where I sit the scene is as complete as in any of the major league baseball parks I have ever attended: the two teams, the stands, the fans, the lights, the vendors, the scoreboard. The only difference is that I sit alone in the left field bleacher and the only player who seems to have substance is Shoeless Joe Jackson. When Joe's team is at bat, the left fielder below me is transparent as if he were made of vapour. He performs mechanically, but seems not to have facial features. We do not converse.

A great amphitheatre of grandstand looms dark against the sky, the park is surrounded by decks of floodlights making it brighter than day, the crowd buzzes, the vendors hawk their wares, and I cannot keep the promise I made myself not to ask Shoeless Joe Jackson about his suspension and what it means to him.

While the pitcher warms up for the third inning we talk.

'It must have been . . . It must have been like . . .' but I can't find the words.

'Like having a part of me amputated, slick and smooth and painless, like having an arm or a leg taken off with one swipe of a scalpel, big and blue as a sword,' and Joe looks up at me and his dark eyes seem about to burst with the pain of it. 'A friend of mine used to tell about the war, how him and a buddy was running across a field when a piece of shrapnel took his friend's head off, and how the friend ran, headless, for several strides before he fell. I'm told that old men wake in the night and scratch itchy legs that have been dust for fifty years. That was me. Years and years later, I'd wake in the night with the smell of the ballpark in my nostrils and the cool of the grass on my feet. The thrill of the grass . . .'

How I wish my father could be here with me. He died before we had television in our part of the country. The very next year he could have watched in grainy black and white as Don Larsen pitched a no-hitter in the World Series. He would have loved hating the Yankees as they won that game. We were always going to go to a major-league baseball game, he and I. But the time was never right, the money always needed for something else. One of the last days of his life, late in the night while I sat with him because the pain wouldn't let him sleep, the radio dragged in a staticky station broadcasting a White Sox game. We hunched over the radio and cheered them on, but they lost. Dad told the story of the Black Sox Scandal for the last time. Told of seeing two of those World Series games, told of the way Shoeless Joe Jackson hit, told the dimensions of Comiskey Park, and how during the series the mobsters in striped suits sat in the box seats with their colourful women, watching the game and perhaps making plans to go out later and kill a rival.

'You must go,' he said. 'I've been in all sixteen major league parks. I want you to do it too. The summers belong to somebody else now, have for a long time.' I nodded agreement.

'Hell, you know what I mean,' he said, shaking his head.

I did indeed.

'I loved the game,' Shoeless Joe went on. 'I'd have played for food money. I'd have played free and worked for food. It was the game, the parks, the smells, the sounds. Have you ever held a bat or a baseball to your face? The varnish, the leather. And it was the crowd, the excitement of them rising as one when the ball was hit deep. The sound was like a chorus. Then there was the chug-a-lug of the tin lizzies in the parking lots and the hotels with their brass spittoons in the lobbies and brass beds in the rooms. It makes me tingle all over like a kid on his way to his first double-header, just to talk about it.'

The year after Annie and I were married, the year we first rented this farm, I dug Annie's garden for her; dug it by hand, stepping a spade into the soft black soil, ruining my salesman's hands. After I finished it rained, an Iowa spring rain as soft as spray from a warm hose. The clods of earth I had dug seemed to melt until the garden leveled out, looking like a patch of black ocean. It was near noon on a gentle Sunday when I walked out to that garden. The soil was soft and my shoes disappeared as I plodded until I was near the centre. There I knelt, the soil cool on my knees. I looked up at the low grey sky; the rain had stopped and the only sound was the surrounding trees dripping fragrantly. Suddenly I thrust my hands wrist-deep into the snuffy-black earth. The air was pure. All around me the clean smell of earth and water. Keeping my hands buried I stirred the earth with my fingers and I knew I loved Iowa as much as a man could love a piece of earth.

When I came back to the house Annie stopped me at the door, made me wait on the verandah, then hosed me down as if I were a door with too many handprints on it, while I tried to explain my epiphany. It is very difficult to describe an experience of religious significance while you are being sprayed with a garden hose by a laughing, loving woman.

'What happened to the sun?' Shoeless Joe says to me, waving his hand toward the banks of floodlights that surround the park.

'Only stadium in the big leagues that doesn't have them is Wrigley Field,' I say. 'The owners found that more people could attend night games. They even play the World Series at night now.'

Joe purses his lips, considering.

'It's harder to see the ball, especially at the plate.'

'When there are breaks they usually go against the ball-players, right? But I notice you're three for three so far,' I add, looking down at his uniform, the only identifying marks a large s with an o in the top crook, an x in the bottom, and an American flag with 48 stars on his left sleeve near the elbow.

Joe grins. 'I'd play for the Devil's own team just for the touch of a baseball. Hell, I'd play in the dark if I had to.'

I want to ask about that day in December, 1951. If he'd lasted another few years things might have been different. There was a move afoot to have his record cleared, but it died with him. I wanted to ask, but my instinct told me not to. There are things it is better not to know.

It is one of those nights when the sky is close enough to touch, so close that looking up is like seeing my own eyes reflected in a rain barrel. I sit in the bleacher just outside the left field fence. I clutch in my hand a hot dog with mustard, onions and green relish. The voice of the crowd roars in my ears like the sea. Chords of the 'Star-spangled Banner' and 'Take Me out to the Ballgame' float across the field. A Coke bottle is propped against my thigh, squat, greenish, the ice-cream-haired elf grinning conspiratorially from the cap.

Below me in left field, Shoeless Joe Jackson glides over the plush velvet grass, silent as a jungle cat. He prowls and paces, crouches ready to spring as, nearly 300 feet away, the ball is pitched. At the sound of the bat he wafts in whatever direction

21

is required as if he were on ball bearings.

Then the intrusive sound of a screen door slamming reaches me, and I blink and start. I recognize it as the sound of the door to my house and looking into the distance, I can see a shape that I know is my daughter toddling down the back steps. Perhaps the lights or the crowd has awakened her and she has somehow eluded Annie. I judge the distance to the steps. I am just to the inside of the foul pole which is exactly 330 feet from home plate. I tense. Karin will surely be drawn to the lights and the emerald dazzle of the infield. If she touches anything, I fear it will all disappear, perhaps forever. Then as if she senses my discomfort she stumbles away from the lights, walking in the ragged fringe of darkness well outside the third-base line. She trails a blanket behind her, one tiny fist rubbing a sleepy eye. She is barefoot and wears a white flannelette nightgown covered in an explosion of daisies.

She climbs up the bleacher, alternating a knee and a foot on each step, and crawls into my lap, silently, like a kitten. I hold her close and wrap the blanket around her feet. The play goes on; her innocence has not disturbed the balance.

'What is it?' she says shyly, her eyes indicating that she means all that she sees.

'Just watch the left fielder,' I say. 'He'll tell you all you ever need to know about a baseball game. Watch his feet as the pitcher accepts the sign and gets ready to pitch. A good left fielder knows what pitch is coming and he can tell from the angle of the bat where the ball is going to be hit and, if he's good, how hard.'

I look down at Karin. She cocks one sky-blue eye at me, wrinkling her nose, then snuggles into my chest the index finger of her right hand tracing tiny circles around her nose.

The crack of the bat is sharp as the yelp of a kicked cur. Shoeless Joe whirls, takes five loping strides directly toward us, turns again, reaches up, and the ball smacks into his glove. The final batter dawdles in the on-deck circle.

'Can I come back again?' Joe asks.

'I built this left field for you. It's yours any time you want to use it. They play 162 games a season now.'

'There are others,' he says. 'If you were to finish the infield, why, old Chick Gandil could play first base, and we'd have the Swede at shortstop and Buck Weaver at third.' I can feel his excitement rising. 'We could stick McMullin in at second, and Cicotte and Lefty Williams would like to pitch again. Do you think you could finish the centre field? It would mean a lot to Happy Felsch.'

'Consider it done,' I say, hardly thinking of the time, the money, the backbreaking labour it entails. 'Consider it done,' I say again, then stop suddenly as an idea creeps into my brain like a runner inching off first base.

'I know a catcher,' I say. 'He never made the majors, but in his prime he was good. Really good. Played Class B ball in Florida and California . . .'

'We could give him a try,' says Shoeless Joe. 'You give us a place to play and we'll look at your catcher.'

I swear the stars have moved in close enough to eavesdrop as I sit in this single rickety bleacher that I built with my unskilled hands, looking down at Shoeless Joe Jackson. A breath of clover travels on the summer wind. Behind me, just yards away, brook water plashes softly in the darkness, a frog shrills, fireflies dazzle the night like red pepper. A petal falls.

'God, what an outfield,' he says. 'What a left field.' He looks up at me and I look down at him. 'This must be heaven,' he says.

'No. It's Iowa,' I reply automatically. But then I feel the night rubbing softly against my face like cherry blossoms; look at the sleeping girl-child in my arms, her small hand curled around one of my fingers; think of the fierce warmth of the woman waiting for me in the house; inhale the freshcut grass smell that seems locked in the air like permanent incense, and listen to the drone of the crowd, as below me Shoeless Joe Jackson tenses, watching the angle of the distant bat for a clue as to where the ball will be hit.

'I think you're right, Joe,' I say, but softly enough not to disturb his concentration.

Arbre de Décision

George Bowering

ARTHUR CUFF TURNED OFF the shower & heard the phone ringing. Grabbing a towel for his hair, he hurried to the hall & lifted
the white receiver. Hello? he said, dripping on the broadloom.
He let it ring & ring while he rubbed his short hair with the
towel. The mirror was all fogged up, so he cleared a space with
the towel, right in front of his face. No, he could get by without
shaving.

Arthur Cuff? askt the crude voice. I've got some news for
you, Arthur. I'm not telling you exactly when it's going to happen, or where, but sometime this week you are going to get the
living shit kickt out of you. You might even wind up a dead
man. I thought you'd like to know.

He almost wisht he had answered the phone. He almost always answered the phone or the door, or letters from people offering to sell things. But he had been warned not to answer the
phone this evening. Maybe he would shave after all.

Arthur? said a small voice, & then a little louder. Arthur, this
is Judy from the office? You were probably kidding, or maybe
you just thought you were kidding, but you said if I was ever
lonely I should just give you a call? He didnt answer right away,
& then the voice went on, without question. I've thought of it
often & said no, & I even dialed your number a few times &
then put the phone down. This time I just didn't put the phone
down.

He imagined Darlene waiting for him in the bedroom. She
was probably smiling right now, her famous smile, having
heard the phone ring God knows how many times, & knowing
that she was more important than anything else, business,
death, other loves, amazing offers. He didnt want to spend the
time shaving.

Who is this? he said, & the towel dropt to his feet. Wouldnt
you fucking like to know? said the brutish voice. Look, you
must have the wrong party, said Arthur Cuff. How many fucking Arthur Cuffs you think there are in the fucking phone book,
Arthur? His jaw workt silently for a while before the words
came out. Please, look, whatever I did to you, I didnt know . . .

I'm sorry . . . cant I do something to clear this up? But he was talking to a dead phone.

It was the first time Judy had spoken to him since he had made that wisecrack to her a week or more ago. That made it strange, & so did this: she had not said anything more than what's usual when one hands a man his mail, but her eyes had lookt as if she were telling him something significant, & when he began on his mail at his desk, the first item was a folded & scotch-taped piece of paper upon which were hand-written the words, Don't answer your telephone tonight.

Well, I'm glad you didnt put it down this time, Judy, he said into the mouthpiece, & I'm glad I decided to pick mine up. You caught me just as I was stepping out of the shower. He heard a light gasp on the other end, & took it to be half-kidding, flirting, a nervous outspokenness. Would you like to meet me somewhere? he askt. She answered with one word. Well then, he said, letting the white towel hang over his shoulder, would you like to come over here, for a drink?

He walkt on the broadloom with his bare feet dry now, the towel around his hips, into the bedroom. Darlene was glimmeringly naked, sitting in half-lotus position on the bed, a white smile in the dim light. He noticed that she had left her clothes in a line that led from the door to the bed, & wondered whether she had done so with particular care. Her long blonde hair curled at the ends, half-hiding the small nipples of her lovely round breasts. I'm so glad you didn't answer the phone, she said.

Look, whoever the hell this is, why dont you go mug little old ladies, which is probably your regular job, said Arthur. You dont know who you're talking too, Cuff, said the crude voice. It sounded like someone five feet tall & four feet wide, in a hat. That's right, & I dont give a damn, said Arthur. Besides, which, it's 'whom', not 'who', you dumb cluck.

He thought he might as well shave after all. It would take no more time to shave than it would have taken to talk to whomever was on the phone. He probably wanted to blunt the little edge of fear that had toucht his naked belly. There had been fear in the voice that had advised him not to answer his phone again tonight. It was a female voice. It sounded a little Greek, but familiar, maybe.

It was true. He *had* been only half-kidding, not expecting much, not because Judy was a great beauty; she wasnt. But office assignations were the stuff of popular sociology — one went thru the language, half-kidding, but one did not really expect a phone call. No, I wasnt kidding, but, uh, he said. You thought you were? she said, asking. No, he said quickly. No, it's just that I wish you'd called last night, or tomorrow. There was no question about it now: I'll leave you my number, she said.

He might as well have taken the time to shave. Or really, there was no reason for the question of shaving to have come up. There he stood, foolishly, a white towel around his suckt-in middle, & there was no one to see his readiness. Darlene had upt & gone while he was in the noise of the shower. There was no sign of her, not a scrap of clothing on the floor, not an indentation on the bed. But yes there was, three numerals followed by a dash followed by four more numerals on a piece of letterhead paper on the glass top of the white dresser.

Arthur stood naked, the white towel on the broadloom at his feet, trying to think. His eyes fell on the handy telephone numbers, & he thought: I'll call the police. He dialled the number, trying to plan what he would say, how to describe the man's voice. It was brutal, but what would the police think of that voice? They could think he was queer. He bent his knees & pickt up the towel, & the policeman's voice was on the line. First Precinct. Officer Pantages speaking. A definite Greek accent.

It was a most unexpected message, & he had no idea whether it was in Judy's handwriting. He always answered his telephone, even getting off the toilet to do so. Could she be planning something nasty or something presumptive because of that remark he had made to her a couple weeks ago? He was reluctant to talk to her, but he had never received such a message before, so he went to the outside office to ask for some, what, clarification. She was nowhere in sight. I havent seen her since I came back from shipping, said Valerie.

In his compromise, the white Pierre Cardin bathrobe over slacks & golf shirt, he opened the hall door just before it would likely ring a second time. Judy was surprisingly pretty. Her light brown hair drifted in soft curls about her face, & her plump lips parted over moist teeth. She was wearing a plum-coloured *crepe de chine* blouse he remembered from the office, but now it plunged open & showed him the promise of adorable girlish contour. Oh, Lord, he thought. Oh, hi, come in, please, he said.

When he reacht the bed Darlene fell gently forward from her

27

half-lotus position, to her knees & one hand. With the other she pulled away the towel, & he spun with the motion, comically, one rotation, till his piece was pointing gently at her. She took his hand & urged him to lie on his back, & in a trice she was above him, in a parody of her Oriental position of a few moments before, a smile on her face half-hidden by the blonde hair falling toward him. Then she tuckt him in quickly, & began that sweetest slide in the world, settling her bright torso down on his hipbones. Oh, you look a happy man, she said, speaking from her throat, & placing four tasty fingers into his mouth.

Listen, sucker, said the short crude voice, I dont give a shit if you're a fucking who or a fucking whom, or a goddamn fucking hoot-owl. I'm interested in what you're *going* to be, & you're going to be half-dead or worse in a day or two, or in your jesus tomb. You made a big mistake when you starting laying your fucking fingers on that woman, Cuff. The man's last consonant turned into a cough, & Arthur shouted: What woman are you talking about? The man said, wouldnt you fucking like to know whom! & sounded as if he were ready to slam down his receiver.

While he was shaving it came to him, & at that moment he lookt into his startled eyes. A half-year ago he had been sitting at the white leather bar of a west-side disco, looking with more & more candour at the reflection of a beautiful woman with long straight black hair & black-rimmed glasses in the mirror. Uncharacteristically he had bought her a drink & started talking with her. Eventually he had taken her to his apartment, & now he remembered her bikini-tanned body & her lilting Greek accent — but he could not remember her name.

The telephone sported one of those gadgets stuck to its side, with a cheap ballpoint pen in it. He pluckt it & held it over a square of paper, upon which he tried not to drip. Okay, shoot, he said. Oh, I'm not going to *shoot* you, Arthur. Her voice was unexpectedly provocative. Even as she recited her number & got him to repeat it, he marvelled that this could be the same Judy from the office, the one in the loose purple shirt. As he put down the receiver & bent to pick up the towel, he noticed his semi-erect piece give a little bob. Was it thinking of Judy or looking forward to the bedroom? He was carrying the paper as he walkt there.

He lookt at the number for a while, as surprise gave way to disappointment. It was hard to tell from so short a sample, especially with numerals, but it lookt like Darlene's handwriting all right. He would have been sure if she'd drawn the number on the mirror with lipstick. Catch me before I fuck again. He dialled the number. A male voice with a slight Greek accent answered. He said he was speaking from the police station.

It was the first time he had ever received a threatening phone call. It was the first time he had received any kind of threat from a stranger, an individual. The man knew his name, too. Could he have got it from the phone book, at random? Even if he had, he could get his address from the same source. Was it some kind of prank someone set up at the office? He put down the dead phone at last, & decided to get dressed fast, in the clothes he had set out for the disco. He would look a little odd, leaving town in white slacks. He threw open the dresser drawers & jammed things into his smaller suitcase.

He decided it was a joke he didnt quite get, or that Judy hadnt quite got right. When he crumpled it up to toss it away, the scotch tape clung to his finger. He had to pick it off with his other hand & hold it over the white waste basket & shake it. Then he pickt it out again & flattened it. Was that Judy's handwriting? Sure it was. He crumpled it up & scraped it off his fingers onto the inside lip of the waste basket. He thought quickly of a nifty remark he would make to her when he left the office that afternoon, & laught softly while he reacht for the top of his mail.

On his way to the hall door he checkt himself out in the mirror over the telephone table. White Cardin bathrobe, dark blue slacks, dark blue golf shirt. Very natty, he decided, opening the door & his mouth at the same time. He had been planning to say something cheerful & slightly suggestive with the latter, but he just kept it open & lookt at the people who had come to his door. One was Judy. She was wearing a sateen warm-up jacket & a matching sateen baseball cap, in maroon & white. The man was short & wide, & while he was not wearing a Bogart hat, he *was* wearing a navy blue knitted cap. What is this? askt Arthur. You mean whom is this, you fucking asshole, said the man.

I don't think I even heard it ringing, he said, taking off the towel & dropping it at the end of her line of clothes. He almost leapt onto the bed, he was so happy to see her healthy body in the low light. He held her length to him, & then rolled till she was on top. But she was having none of that, & continued the roll. Oh, all right, he said to himself, whatever. She was on her knees & he was behind her. What a lovely white bum reacht up to him. He offered to enter her, & did, only till he had acquired her wetness. Then her hand reacht beneath them & led him to her higher aperture, while her lips flext to make her meaning a part of the room. Are you a Greek? he askt, & she laught, pushing back against him.

It's whom, is it? You pickt a great time to come on pedantic, Cuff. The word surprised Arthur. He didnt know how to revise his image of a squat hoodlum in a hat. It is not pedantry to ask for a simple correct pronoun reference, he said. Well listen, Cuff, the whole idea of correctness in such matters is definitely pedantry. Grammarians are interested in usage nowadays, & nowadays 'who' is a respected usage in such cases. In any case, it is not the rules of grammar that are going to be busted, Cuff. Arthur couldnt resist: I presume that you mean 'broken', he said.

He could think of no Greek woman who would be likely to know his phone number. It was quite likely that the fear in the voice had been real, but he decided that the Greek accent had been faked. In any case it was the fear, not the accent, that had convinced him not to answer his phone this evening. But why Greek? A fake Greek accent was at least as puzzling as a real Greek accent. Why didnt she fake an Italian accent? Or a Chinese one? & on the subject of fake voices, could it have been a man faking a woman's voice? Could the fear have been faked, after all, in order to instill some fear in him? If the phone were to ring again, should he answer it this time, to find out something, at least?

Okay, terrific, he said, finding a square white piece of paper. But there was no pen or pencil beside the telephone. There never was when you needed one. Judy pronounced her number in a happy sing-song voice. But the nearest pen was in the bedroom. The only pen he could think of was in the bedroom. You got it? askt Judy. He was not about to go in there, & back out to the phone. It wasnt worth the risk. Look, Judy, he said, I'll see you in the office tomorrow. How about if we go to dinner tomorrow night? Judy agreed, & added: & Arthur? I know this disco, you'll love it, I think it's called the West Side? Now *he* agreed, half-heartedly, perhaps.

He stood foolishly in his towel, a mid-city Tarzan looking at a phone number he had never seen before. It seemed to be jotted by Darlene's hand, but it wasnt her number, not the one he knew, anyway. But what else could he do? He dialled the number. Hello, someone said, not helping much. Hello, this is Arthur Cuff; who am I talking to? The male voice said: I am just a simple immigrant from Greece, but I know that in English you say 'whom' as the object of the preposition, & you shouldnt end a sentence with a preposition. Arthur didnt know what to believe, for the voice betrayed no trace of an accent.

Officer Pantages, he said, I want to report a threat on my life. God, the way he had said it, the voice he heard coming from himself — the cop *would* think he was queer. But Constable Pantages went thru his regular desk-officer routine, drawing a description of the offending voice (Arthur couldnt think of a way of telling him he thought the hood was wearing a hat) & the kind of language used. He said the living shit? Are you sure? The phrase somehow sounded more authentic, more street-wise, coming wrapt-up in a slight Greek accent. We know about this guy, I'm afraid, Mr. Cuff, said the voice. I think you had better take him seriously. We dont know how many people he calls, but he *does* follow thru with his threats. A couple times he has killed people. How do you know, thought Arthur, & then he felt cold, or was it just more aware, in his nakedness.

Thank you, Valerie, he said. Should I tell her you want to see her, she askt, imitating an all-business secretary, but making it clear that she was doing so. No, it's all right, it's nothing, he said. Okay, she said, & on turning away, she made her first step toward him, so that her breast, loose inside a white muslin blouse, bumpt against his upper arm. He looked at her, distraction replaced by what his mother used to call distraction when he was at business school.

Had he maneuvered Judy into the bedroom, or had she led him there? It had begun when she took off her pumps just inside the hall door. Now here she was, feathery brown hair & alert naked body, sitting like no office help on the edge of the bed. He thought he would bend for one kiss before he took off his white bathrobe, but as he did so, she put her small hand on the back of his skull & continued his descent, till his surprised head was between her short thighs. I'm so glad I called at last, she said, & let the top half of her body fall back onto the bed. He gave one long preparatory lick. There was only a slight flavour, unfamiliar & pleasant.

I am a very happy man, he said, speaking around the fingers in his mouth. Darlene lifted her white chin toward the ceiling & let her blonde hair fall free behind her. Up & down she rode, & forward & back. He lay perfectly still except for the two hands he lifted to hold her breasts. She had now taken her fingers from his mouth & was using them just above the place where

31

she held him. All at once she suckt some air & exclaimed: ἀγλαοζ ἀλάου τόρη Περσεφνετα, & a half-second later he archt & cried, Eureka!

Dont hang up on me, you illiterate slob, said Arthur, glad to be a phoning distance, but enjoying his own ardour. At least tell me what woman upon whom I am supposed to have laid my fingers. There was a silence that Arthur planned to describe as ominous when he got the chance, sure to come soon, he hoped. Then the short muscular behatted voice proved still to be there. It's too late for youm to worry about that, Cuff (& the voice was truly frightening now, because there was hurt in it) because you laid your fingers & a lot more on Judy, & Judy is mine, that's whom's, & I am going to lay a fuckin knife in under your ribs, & you are going to die for me with your nice three-piece big businessman suit on. Now he did hang up.

As he lookt into the mirror & tried to remember her name, a Greek name, obviously, he filled his hand with lather & held his half-erect piece, Diana, or Helena, or, he was looking into the mirror but seeing her long straight black hair & there were her black horn-rimmed glasses against his chest as she set her teeth on his nipple, Semiramis, foam-born, she had wide white teeth in front, he squeezed as he pulled & her name did not come, but he would try again later.

He noticed two things simultaneously on arriving in the bedroom — an odor of pecans, necessarily faint, & the back of Darlene's body. She was lying face down on the white counterpane, her feet together, her arms reaching beyond her head. A series of curved lines lying straight. He liked the rise of her buttocks, beginning a view of a woman of two perfect halves. He was glad the subdued light pickt out the indentation along her spine & then the trace of ribs. What a healthy body, he thought. He went to the dresser, put down the square of white paper, & pickt up the bottle of baby oil. But when he approacht the bed, Darlene sat up & took the bottle from him. She deftly pulled the towel from his loins & began to rub him with Johnson & Johnson.

What was he going to say? That he called this number because he was curious? The accented & purportedly constabulary voice began the routine so familiar from cop movies. Arthur, before he quite knew it, had given his name, address, & phone number. By then he thought it was too late to say there was no reason for calling. I would like to report a missing person, I guess, he said. The policeman did not seem to find his language

32

odd at all. You talking about Darlene? Now the voice was a little threatening. Then it was a good deal more threatening. So I know where you live at last, you fucker, it said. Now, wait a minute, I didn't —, began Arthur. Mr. Cuff; I am going to be off duty in twenty-four minutes. Then I will begin to kill you, Mister. You know how? Arthur did not ask. I am going to kill you the way we Greeks do it in our ritualistic way, when it is a matter of jealous passion.

Not wanting to trust the telephone even to call a taxi, he rusht down to the street in his silly white disco outfit, & as luck would have it, managed to flag down a cab right away. The speed with which the car negotiated the thruway to the airport reassured him quite a lot. In fact, maybe he was over-reacting. But here he was, making a big deal of it — what would the driver say if he told him he'd changed his mind? Well, cabbies are used to everything you can imagine. He would take the first plane that was not going north. There was a moving van in front of them, braking hard & turning sideways & falling over on its side, & they couldnt stop at this speed. They were crashing fast into the overturning truck.

He was just about to open the first letter on the pile, when his phone buzzed. Valerie's voice instructed that it was line one he might listen to, & he pusht the button, to hear a loud voice already half-way thru a sentence. It was a tough voice with a strong accent. Greek, perhaps: . . . bastard. We learned how to take care of guys like you, bigshot, think you can have anything you want, you just got to snap your fingers. Arthur got him while he was taking a breath. Who is this, please? But the breathtaker was not a listener. You got to go to slip sometime, & when you do you're going to wake up dying, you bastard. That apartment building of yours will be nothing but ashes, & you will be a few ashes in the ashes. He apparently slammed his receiver down, not in the mood for receiving. Hold my calls, Valerie, said Arthur.

The man with the knitted cap let Judy do the pushing, & followed her into the apartment. What the hell is this? demanded Arthur. But Judy just said, In the bathroom, Art, & this time the fellow did the pushing. The mirror was no longer steamed up, & in it he saw the fellow take a short braided whip from inside his leather jacket. Clothes off, Art, said Judy, removing her cap, & shaking her soft brown hair. When he stood in his white shorts, she pointed at them. When he had taken them off, she spoke again. On your knees, Art. Head over the toilet.

33

He pusht into her slowly, a very little bit deeper each time, his hands enjoying their hold on her hipbones. That's my doggy, she said, grunting a little. He loved the little slap of his hips against her buttocks. His piece did hurt, each push hurt without deterring his excitement. Darlene began to pant noticeably. Good doggy, she said, you're, a good, good, doggy. Her hair was spilled forward over her face, & he could see high up the back of her neck, a delicacy. He wondered whether he could lean forward & give her a little bite there. Speak, she said. I love you, Darlene, he said, puffing. No, she said, speak. Good doggy. He plunged, deep, into his relief. Wwooof! he called. Whhoof, woof!

How much, said the still-gruff voice, how much use is your vaunted correctness of grammar going to be to you while you are looking down the barrel of a .38 revolver? This is crazy, thought Arthur, I thought he was just going to beat the shit out of me, & now he's going to shoot me, & I dont even know why he was going to beat the shit out of me. Are you saying you're going to shoot me? he askt. You fucking got it, whom. The hat was back on the threatener. But why? The answer was not really satisfactory: Because I cant stand a fucking pedant!

If the Greek accent was faked & the fear was also faked, & the femininity of the voice was not faked, what then? The accent would be faked because the speaker was a woman he knew well, & she was interested in fabricating mystery. Why do people do that? To flirt. But why flirt with fear? To titillate him — he would hear another installment soon, he was sure of that. Whoever it was, she was creating an elaborate seduction during which the allurement would be laced with the thrill of danger. He recalled the time he had made it with what was her name in the all-night laundry room in the basement of her apartment building, she & her husband's apartment building. An image of white machines passed around his head. But how how could he aid in this scenario? Should he answer the telephone if it rang again?

Who was that on the phone? askt Darlene, when he finally got to the bedroom. He stood beside the bed, hoping she would remove the towel, but she just lay on her side, her head held by one hand up, elbow on pillow, blonde hair falling down the whiteness of her arm. He took off the towel & folded it, placing it beside a square of paper on the dresser. It was just someone from the office, he said. You spend too much time thinking about the office, said Darlene. He smiled an agreement to the statement & to the implied remedy, & lay beside her, impatient but willing to spend a little time nuzzling her upper body. It was not long till compliant Darlene was holding his buttocks, pulling him into her again & again, but Arthur had his eyes closed, thinking of brown-haired Judy, who was saying, Please no, no, oh uh, yes. Darlene was making no sound whatsoever.

I'll finish a sentence with a preposition any time I want to, & let me inform you that a grammar lesson is not what I'm phoning for, said Arthur. There you go again, said the accentless voice. What are you after? askt Arthur. You phoned me, said the purported Greek. I was just about to enjoy a little in & out, when this damned phone rang, & by the time I got to the battle stations again, she was gone & your phone number was the only thing around, said Arthur. I might have known, said the modulated voice — you know, speech with which the speaker is not careful is very much like degenerate sex. It is an injury against a lovely gift. That is exactly how the Greek democracy fell. Arthur tried not to sound querulous: Would you please tell me where Darlene has gotten to? There was a sigh on the phone: then: I'm afraid I cannot put up with this any longer. Off I am going to have to ring.

Listen, Officer Pantages, he said, trying not to sound like a disco queen, this has never happened to me before, but I've had a threat upon my life. What a stupid phrase, he thought. The policeman gave no aural sign that he found anything peculiar about the language, though. He simply askt the routine questions. Arthur tried to wrap the towel around his waist with one hand. The knuckles of the other were white with his grip on the phone. You're sure he said I thought you'd like to know? No need to worry. We know this guy. He tries to get you to sound scared because it gets him off. He pulls his wire while you're on the phone. Arthur was relieved, he guessed. Thank you. As he was hanging up he wondered what the cop would think of *that* phrase.

If Valerie was half-way telling the truth, & why not, Judy must have left the office right after handing him the note. He walkt quickly back thru the open door into his own office & over to the window. She might be on the sidewalk below, just getting into a car. He threw the window open & leaned his head & trunk out into the sudden white light. Someone grabbed his ankles & in one quick motion lifted him up & out, into the noise, four stories above a number of moving strangers.

Almost before he had finisht his invitation, Judy was not only inside the apartment but in his arms, on tiptoes, the plum blouse & its gorgeous contents pressed against him. After a long open kiss, which she must have been saving up for heaven knows how long at the office, he said: Would you like a drink? Right out of the movies. But she must have been seeing another kind of movie, at least in her fancy. No, she said, & the word said more. He accordingly took her small hand in his & led her toward the chaste white door of his bedroom. Once inside, she lookt the room over slowly, & that was alluring, & then she sat down in the chair in front of his dresser. Would you do a favour for me, she askt. That's what I'm here for, he replied, a male if there ever was one. I'd love it if you would take your clothes off first, she said, her eyes wide open, flirting eyes looking up at him & then down. No sooner said than done, he said. He couldnt help seeing himself in the mirror as he became naked in the soft light. When he was fully naked he prepared himself to walk toward her attired & seated promise, but she had a revolver pointed straight at his suckt-in belly.

Forward & back she rockt, up & down, cowgirl Darlene, & each time she leaned forward her sumptuous breasts bobbed toward one another. I am indeed a happy man, he said, tasting her departed fingers. She squeezed & rockt & once in a while wiggled sideways, & his knees lifted behind her. Ah heh, ah heh, aheh eh, she said, & her eyes were tight closed as her chin lifted high, & she shuddered while he watcht, she came in full view while he held still as a bridge. She settled back down on him, heavily, & in another half-minute she said: I'm going to have a cigarette. He tried to hold her there. But I havent come, I'm almost, would you? She lifted herself right off. Please, he askt. Oh Arthur, she replied from the other side of the room, why dont you drop dead?

Yes, I would like to know whom, & I am glad you got your pronoun right this time. If I am going to be accused of laying my fingers on a woman, & if I am going to be threatened for so doing, the least the accuser & threatener can do is to tell me which woman it is I have fingered. He felt rather a bit pleased by his sentence, not characteristic of fear nor of anger. But now Mr. Short & Wide came back: Okay, lover man, I'm going to tell you. If the name Darlene rings a bell, I'm Darlene's special friend, & whether I am a who or a whom, I am talking to thou, & I am telling you that when you meet me you are going to find out what it is like to have some fingers on you, & then you are going to find out what it's like to have a prick in you, if you dont already know. Now Arthur was just beginning to feel fear at last.

He could not remember her name, but he could not forget her dark-rimmed glasses. The frames were wide & shallow, & her eyes large & dark behind them. He remembered with pleasure the way her glasses slipt half-way down her nose, even while he remembered with revulsion her pleasure in bruising his flesh. From her traditional Greek market bag she had taken scarf after particoloured scarf, & as he lay on his back his piece had risen against his belly while she leaned forward in her white undergarments, tying his wrists & ankles to the bed. In his mouth she had stuft a white scarf, & as she used the little metallic things to hit him two hundred times, perspiration broke out all over her body & face, till the glasses fell from her & landed on his thigh, so that she was hitting down blindly, an owl, & in a stage whisper shouting: ουτοζ εστιυ Αρσυωυ, εηδζπόσζ, υεκσζ δε τξσδε δεζιαζ, εργου δικαίαζ τεκτουζ.

He should not have carried the little square of paper into the bedroom with him. Darlene was standing, nude except for white high heels, at the window, looking out at the park across the street. Light played upon her body from several directions, & he retained his half-erection. Who was that? she askt as she turned to face him. Oh, someone from the office, he said, casually perhaps, dropping the paper on the dresser, She walkt in that lovely woman way on her high heels over to the dresser, & pickt up the paper, reading the number there. He wisht he had dript all over it. She burst awkwardly into fury, pulling off one shoe. You god damn son of a bitch, bastard! She shriekt, her hair flying as she lunged at him, swinging. What are you doing with Judy? She drove her spike heel at his face as he fell toward the bed.

Arthur had given his name & address before he'd thought to wonder whether he should believe that he was talking to a policeman. The Greek voice surprised him now: Did Darlene leave this number? He admitted that she had, & askt where she was. She's over at our place, of course. Why dont you come over? said the putative cop. I'm not sure I want to, said Arthur. Oh, but we want you to, right now, was the answer, & it sounded like a threat. Now what should he do, call the cops? What for? was his lame response. Oh, a little costume fun, said the Greek, & it didnt matter whether he was a policeman or not. Darlene is going to be a motorcycle cop, all black leather, & I'm going to be a highway rapist, & guess what you're going to be? Arthur lookt at the slightly rumpled white sheets. A motorcycle? There was just a *soupcon* of silence. Very cute, Arthur. Now here'e the address . . .

The second he was on the sidewalk, suitcase in hand, jacket of his white suit unbuttoned, why did he wear his shirt open with two gold chains hanging in his chest hair, there was a taxi at the curb, & he stept right in, asking for the airport & leaning back against the centre of the rear seat, his arms flung out to the sides. He didnt notice anything but the movement of the cab, windows flying by, & then no windows, they were driving thru the park, & now stopping with some water before them, the vehicle poking its nose down & then up, as the driver got out & then opened the back door on the left side. He had always wondered where he would die, but putting up a struggle was better than just dying in a taxi in the park. But before he could negotiate a violent movement he saw that the cab driver was wearing rectangular black-framed eyeglasses. It was the slim Greek woman from the disco. Oh God, hello, Irena, he said. My name is Elena, she said, ducking her head as she came in, reaching with her tapered fingers for his whiteness.

He had just pickt up the top item from his pile of mail, when the phone buzzed. Valerie said he should attend to line three, so he deprest the appropriate button & said his name into the mouthpiece, meanwhile fishing a white folded letter from a light grey envelope. How *are* you, *Mr.* Cuff? A tingle went out of the back of his collar & up under his hair. It was the voice of that Greek girl in the disco. Well, hello . . . there. What a surprise, he said, dropping the letter back on the pile. I have decided not to wait for your call, came the sweetly accented voice, but to invite you to my little place for dinner. Can you come tomorrow night? Now there were additional tingles, here & there. I certainly can. May I bring some wine? Red or white? What will we be eating? There was a haughty giggle. You might be surprised. Do you prefer Greek or French?

The foulmouthed hood in the knitted cap was, though short, quite scary, & before he knew it Arthur had taken a backward step. The visitors took that opportunity to walk into the apartment & close the door behind them. In the midst of his alarm, he could still reflect that Judy lookt cute in her baseball cap. No, actually, I do mean what is this, he had the gumption to say. This is a threesome, dear, said Judy, opening her bag & shaking out a frilly white peignoir. You are going to treat me gentle, &

38

he is going to treat me rough. *Comprende?* Nothing like this had ever occured to Arthur.

Darlene made a feminine grunt each time he thrust into her tight loveliness, & when he came with a jolt & an exclamation, she fell prostrate on the fragrant bed, & he stretcht totally upon her healthy body, his face in her abundant hair, now glistening with perspiration. He was waiting for his breath to come back, but managed to gasp out: Oh, I am a happy man. A voice deeper than his said: You're a fucking dead man! Between the door & the bed there was a short but very broad man in a dark suit & a fedora. He was approaching, preparing to swing a baseball bat. How would it be possible to get off her in time & get away from that fully-clothed man?

If you were not quite so much a pedant I could learn to like you, Cuff, said the puzzling man on the phone. Make up your mind, said Arthur archly. Did you call me up to threaten me, liberalize my grammar, or because you were lonely? He heard, in the middle of his pleasant bravado, a rhythmic sound thru the receiver at his ear. It was breath, & became groaning, & was again breath. Well, said the man, now sounding a little taller, perhaps, the first two were necessary & the last was half-right. I've been whacking my duff, Cuff. I just came all over the phone. It took Arthur a while, but he did wonder: is that possible?

If it had been an authentic Greek woman's voice, & if the fear had been authentic as well, would there be any point in not answering the phone? Certainly, now that he had decided that at least two of those factors had been faked, there was no point. But that was all academic in any case, because the phone had not rung all night. It was time to practise some resolution. He decided to imagine the phone ringing & his forthright action. He said ring ring ring in his head, strode to the phone & pickt up the white receiver. Well, hello, said a real woman's voice, though its Greek accent might have been faked. What? askt Arthur. I am so happy that you pickt up the phone in spite of my warning, she said, & he heard a click, presumably her plastic frames striking the bakelite. What? he repeated. Your action demonstrates a certain courage I was hoping to see, she said. What I have in mind for you is an erotic experience — you dont mind my frankness, do you? — that will make anything you have done so far seem utterly domestic in comparison. Arthur searcht for a word. What? he said. How do you feel about women helicopter pilots? she askt.

He was still thinking of Judy's forwardness as he walkt to the bedroom, adjusting the towel. Dinner would be fine, a nice preamble, but he would have to talk her out of the disco. He had never been to a disco in his life. He hated the idea of the language, all that mindless repetition of half-sentences. When he stept into the bedroom and saw Darlene, he forgot language altogether. She was standing beside the bed, wearing baby-blue silk garterbelt & stockings. The towel fell spontaneously from him, & in no time she had him supine on the shag rug, her slippery silk knees touching his ears. He spread his hands on the small of her back, to pull her to his open mouth, but she held back, to speak. I heard everything you said on the phone. I'll see you in the *office* tomorrow, sweetie. She put both her hand around the front of his throat. I could kill you, Arthur, she said.

You are right, according to the old rules of grammar of course, said Arthur. But you should know that that rule about prepositions was made up by early grammarians who thought they could arrest the slide of European civilization by drafting English regulations in compliance with Latin, in which tongue it is of course impossible to finish a sentence with a preposition. It is also impossible, in Latin, to split an infinitive. In English the infinitive has managed to of course come in two halves. The accentless Greek's voice had been trying to interpolate during the last three phrases. But surely you have noticed that the revisions of those rules in our time are made principally by louts who neither read worthwhile books nor observe respectable decorum in any social intercourse, said the cultured foreigner. I will gladly admit that even in my office, where Mammon is chief deity, I never allow myself the employment of the vernacular, said Arthur. What does this have to do with lovely white-breasted Darlene, he wondered. Just so, said the polite stranger in his ear. You agree with me that if we do not preserve the rules of discourse, our literature, bequeathed to us & ordered for us by the Greeks, will be murdered by us. Arthur was all at once aware of his unaccompanied nakedness. He thought about the word. Murdered?

Mythical Beasts

James Ross

EVERYONE IS TAKING a long time to settle down. It is confusing the chairman; eventually it will make him angry or perhaps even throw him into complete disarray. It is always like this — not only at our conventions, but at everyone's. Many of us see each other only once or twice a year, and always want to talk instead of listen.

Still. He has his job to do. Opening remarks are rituals, and this group especially should tolerate them.

'Madam President, Honoured Guests, Ladies and Gentlemen.'

There is a burst of applause from the group that arrived early and spent the afternoon in the bar. Perhaps we should be more selective about memberships; as it is now, all someone has to do is pay his ten dollars a year. We should have a test of knowledge, and one of civilized behaviour.

'Our group is surely well acquainted with our opening speaker, a man of considerable erudition and talent. It is most appropriate that he has consented to address this year's annual conference, and tomorrow, to partake in a panel discussion in the morning, and lead a study group in the afternoon. That study group, incidentally, is fully subscribed, and has been almost since the news of our guest's participation in this year's conference was first announced.'

Like all chairman's remarks, a strange mixture. Obsequious, deferent, pompous, informative. I have been approached twice to handle the job; the next time I will accept. I will likely adopt the same tone, no matter that I hate it.

'But what we owe Mr. Davies most of all is not thanks for the hours of good reading we have all enjoyed. The interests of this organization being what they are, we should fervently thank Mr. Davies for making a wider public aware of the concerns we have shared for many years now. For it is his introduction of the Manticore, a hitherto little known beast from a little studied mythology, and his revelation of its importance to an English speaking audience, that has drawn us together.'

I can't blame him, the Chairman. We thrived on our exclusiveness and our esoteric knowledge for so many years. It was all we had. No notices of our conferences in the papers, a struggling magazine, haphazardly edited and cheaply printed for our articles, no recognition of our best scholars by the majority of the academic community, few new members each year. Perhaps we all want public recognition.

'Born into a humble family.'

Yes, we all were, at least most of us. If we were rich, would we even be aware of mythology?

'For many years the editor . . . During those years he first wrote and published . . .'

Most of us know all this. But would it be possible for a chairman to say that? You all know, etc., and on with it. But here we deal in what everyone knows but does not know, surfaces that are depths, banalities which might really be profundities, endless complications of simplicities. Perhaps he has taken the only way open. Perhaps.

Finally, it is the speaker's turn. And he is perfect, just as he was expected to be. Magic, illusion, theatricality, religion, evil, Jung, Freud, that wonderful scene in the cave. We are wildly enthusiastic, we applaud furiously. He even rises again to make a few more remarks.

ONE ENCHANTED EVENING

IN VARIOUS ROOMS, bottles and glasses and ice in abundance are passed around large groups. We talk and talk. It is good to have a heated disagreement with someone you've just met; good to have some variations on opinions, to hear some ideas you haven't encountered before. Even the quirky ones that seem so off base you'd never consider them make some kind of sense at two in the morning. We are all tired.

A pretty girl. She has said little. 'How many have a sting in their tail, though? When an animal waves its tail, we take it as a sign of happiness or friendliness. Yet we must guard against being too close to the tail; it is dangerous otherwise.'

The group breaks up soon after. Other groups are doing the same. The corridors and elevators are filled with mythologists, most at least half drunk, staggering to their rooms.

WE HAVE AN HOUR long general discussion each morning to take care of small bits of information and business. Today some of our new patrons are introduced; I recognize only one of them. He is the importer of cheap supposedly Aztec statues that are imitations of the stones on Easter Island. I have seen many of them in the homes of acquaintances. His interest in us baffles me, although possibly it is genuine. I'm certain he has sold none of his wares to us. As a group, even as individuals, we would recognize them for what they were. It is, after all, our avocation and most of us pursue it with a certain degree of intensity and skill. So far our field has attracted a few dilettantes. So far. But I notice today that some reporters have been in and out. Perhaps it is because Davies is here; he is important, therefore we must be at least worth a passing glance.

'I wish to move that the name of the Society be changed.' The speaker is one I have seen at conferences before although I've never spoken to him. 'Although it expresses our aims, and clearly indicates our nature, it is a clumsy and awkward name. It might even be what is preventing us from receiving the recognition and publicity we deserve. The press, after all, uses space in such a way.'

But he is interrupted by a chorus of dissent, some from people who originally helped to form the Society, some from those who do not want public recognition, some in the form of a denunciation of the press in general.

Finally the young man regains the floor. 'But our name is so ungainly, so old fashioned.' And this raises another chorus. But he is in command for the time being. '*The Society for the Study and Preservation of Mythical Beasts* is clumsy and long winded,' he reiterates. 'In the academic community, it causes raised eyebrows. I have even been snickered at when I mention my membership.'

But he is interrupted again, this time by the pretty girl I noticed last night. 'We are not here to seek popularity,' she says. 'When I joined, only two years ago, it was by chance, through a marginal note in Frazer. I had to track down everyone who had borrowed the book until I found the one who had made the original note.' She turned, searched the crowd until she saw me. 'It was a reference to one of Dr. Walton's articles in the

43

Journal,' she said, and smiled. I smiled back and nodded encouragement, then she continued. 'Even when I found the writer of the note, he was reluctant to talk to me until he was sure my interest was genuine. But of course, when he discovered it was, he urged me to join, which I did. I am satisfied that we are doing the right thing,' she finished. 'I urge everyone to vote against any motion for a change of title.' She sat down to scattered but vigorous applause, and an undertone of agreement. She had done well.

The young man arose for his final plea. 'Something that will identify us by letters, something like PMLA,' he pleaded. 'SSPMB is ridiculous. Not readily identifiable.'

Ridiculous was the wrong word, too strong. And he had no ideas for an alternative name, although he wanted an acronym.

'I merely wanted the membership to consider it,' he said. 'I would hope that within the year a new title could be devised.'

But he has lost his case now, and has begun to realize it. He slumps back into his seat, looking gloomily around for partisans. But there are very few.

We break for coffee, then our morning discussion groups. The girl sits in on mine, as does the young man who raised the issue. No one says much; in spite of everything I can do, the discussion is torpid. The quarrel has upset everyone.

Lunch is not good. Someone has decided on thematic dishes. The sauce, for instance, is labelled as being used by a legendary Indonesian, that sort of thing. It is a bad sign; we will be naming local chapters after our beasts if we are not careful.

However, things improve in the afternoon. Someone in the group has prepared a paper linking some Southwestern American Indian legends with some middle European ones, apparently by way of Mexico. It stimulates a lively discussion, hampered slightly because the reader of the paper is somewhat of a socialist, and unwilling to give away too much. He has not published yet. The girl says a few words, then speaks to me after the group breaks up. On impulse I invite her to dinner, away from the convention.

It is a success; we are late for the evening speech. I put my ear to the closed banquet room doors, and guess that he is about half finished.

Instead of making a conspicuous entry, we decide to spend the remainder of the evening in my room. She is sharing hers with another delegate, and we agree that it would be foolish to be disturbed.

DAY THREE: SYMBOLIC UNDERCURRENTS AND OTHER SIDE ISSUES

ANNE IS BESIDE ME this morning; we have decided to be open. Although she is considerably younger — twenty two as compared to my thirty four — age is not a problem. I am not married; there is nothing to hide from anyone.

We have barely finished with some business details when Richard Branscombe gets up to speak. He is a quiet person, Richard, and this is obviously a strain for him. So I will listen carefully, what he says will be interesting. Important too, perhaps.

'The addition of *and Symbolic* to our title,' he pauses, looks around at the audience 'whatever form our organization's name might eventually take,' and receives a delighted ripple of laughter, 'would greatly enlarge our scope and increase our flexibility.'

He pauses again, then continues. 'One of our greatest problems in the past has been that some of the texts and materials we have dealt with have been inaccessible to many members, and the cost of reproducing and distributing materials has been a hardship. Often it was impossible to do even this much. Therefore, Mr. Chairman, I propose that we enlarge our scope to include the study of beasts that have symbolic, even if not strictly mythological, value. I would like to hear discussion on this.' Richard takes his seat.

He has struck a nerve, it seems. There is an undercurrent of murmuring throughout the hall. Anne is agitated at the turn the discussion is taking, scribbles notes in shorthand, which I can't read. She whispers angrily to me, then to her neighbour on the left.

'We deal often in oral traditions,' another man is saying. He appears to be about forty-five, perhaps fifty. 'And this means travelling all over the world. Enjoyable as it was when we were younger, my wife and I now find it a hardship, especially with the long distances and the many languages involved. It would be pleasant for many of us to be able to continue our interest at home by reading books.'

Voices rise in agreement. The motion is gathering support.

Another man, about the same age, takes the floor. 'There is

the expense as well,' he says. 'For those of us who have children in college, it is considerable sacrifice to carry out the necessary investigations.'

'Perhaps if the society were to establish a grant system,' a voice from the floor cuts in.

The chairman interrupts. 'It is out of the question. We simply do not have the required financial resources.'

'Perhaps one of the foundations,' is another suggestion.

'They do not consider our work of public benefit. It seems to have no practical application. I have tried several times to get grants, but I have always failed.' That carries weight. Adams is one of our best, very thorough, very erudite. I too have failed to extract money from several foundations, and I rise and mention this. It too has its effect. But in a few minutes, I am sorry I spoke; it was a mistake. It produced the feeling that I agree with Richard's motion, whereas I am against it. I must make this clear, but it will be difficult, for Richard and his allies have raised good points. Opinion is favouring them.

'You must make them change their minds,' Anne whispers angrily in my ear. 'It would be a dreadful mistake if the motion were passed.'

'Yes, of course I must try.' I borrow her pad and pencil, jot down notes. When there is a lull, I speak slowly and carefully, anxious to create the impression that I have thought about all this before. I keep my voice low and hesitant.

'It is indeed tempting. And as I'm sure we all realize, the beasts, the objects and the actions to which our artists give symbolic value are chosen with care. And of course, they speak of values and attitudes, and of often unconscious cultural patterns similiar to those with which we concern ourselves here.'

There are murmurs of agreement.

'However, in spite of their obvious value and richness, I wish to oppose the motion. I am sure Richard has thought about this a great deal; he is not a person who acts according to whim.'

I realize even as I say this that it might well be a key to gaining sympathy. 'It is true that symbols not only add depth and richness to art. They also reveal much — just as mythology does — about the unconscious mind, about man's vast inner world. However, ultimately it is the concern of this society with the beasts that man invents for himself, not those of the natural world to which he pays homage. Many of these symbols are too obvious — I think immediately of lions. Others are simply inaccurate, for instance the linking of the snake and the devil. For these reasons, and for the subsidiary one that many scholars in many organizations and journals have done considerable work in explicating symbolism, I suggest it would be a mistake — a serious mistake — to enlarge our scope at this time.'

I sit down, smiling thoughtfully. Anne starts to applaud loyally. At first she is alone, but after a few claps, isolated pockets of applause spring up. It quickly dies down, but I feel that I have, if not averted the crisis, at least given them something to think about.

And I am right. After a bit more discussion, the motion fails to carry. Not because of votes against, but because of abstentions.

'We will write on the subject in the *Journal*,' Richard says to me, after the group breaks for coffee. 'A forum. Equal space for each side, a lot of room for letters to the editor. Do you approve?'

'Of course, Richard. It's the only way.'

'Shall we have lunch, then?'

'I'd be delighted.'

'You two go ahead,' Anne says. 'I want to copy these notes before I forget what you both said.'

Richard and I are flattered; consequently we enjoy our lunch and our discussion immensely.

DAY FOUR: A SUMMARY

THE LAST DAY. It has been a success and I am especially glad I attended this year. Anne will accompany me to a rented cottage in the Berkshires for a month before she returns to school. We will likely not see much of each other during the year because of distance, so this will be a pleasant interlude.

THANKSGIVING WEEKEND: MISCONCEPTIONS

WE HAVE MET halfway, more or less in the middle of the continent. The hotel is secluded, near a civilized woods which has no underbrush. The leaves have finished falling for the year, but there are many pines so it is neither stark nor depressing the way a deciduous forest would be. There is a small lake. The weather is perfect, and we spend most of our reunion outdoors, walking. We even have a picnic and wade for a short while in

47

the little lake. Although the water is icy cold, it is clear, and the interlude is enjoyable enough.

'I've developed an interest in the unicorn. I'm going to write something, probably a story for children.' She is anxious, wants me to approve of her project.
   I hesitate to encourage her.
   'Well, what's wrong? Tell me.'
   'The unicorn has been very popular.' I try to choose words carefully, am unwilling to insult her. 'There are too many misconceptions about the unicorn. There are already books about it; there are even songs. The true unicorn has been lost, I think.'
   'Maybe I can straighten out some of the misconceptions.'
   'Perhaps you can.' It is more likely that she will fall prey to them, but I won't say this. I won't spoil our weekend or her plans.

CHRISTMAS & NEW YEAR: A COLD OBSERVATION PLATFORM

IT HAS BEEN a trying and unsatisfactory time. She is old enough now to stay away from home for Christmas, but she refuses. And after all, she has younger brothers and sisters who can carry out the traditional visit home. I spent two days at her home, under the guise of being one of her professors who was passing through, and the experience was unnerving. The family is boisterous, the two brothers interested only in football and other contact sports, the parents rather uncritically proud of everything the children do. And I was made rather an exhibition of, I fear. I met too many people, too briefly, had too many superficial conversations. They are all enwrapped in their myth, but have not shown sufficient interest or detachment to study it. Usually I am able to avoid such people.
   This motel room is unsatisfactory as well. And the local library, which seems to be closed most of the time, has a limited selection. Why did I not remember to bring some work to do? She can only sneak away for a few hours a day, and we have been to dinner once.
   I have seen the rough draft of her unicorn story; which seems now to be intended for adults such as her parents. I don't like it, although I don't think I'll tell her yet. She is still too involved in it to see its weaknesses. I will ask her to send me a final copy and make my comments then.

She is barely able to escape from her awful family long enough to accompany me to the airport. They are asking a lot of questions, she says. Male acquaintances who usually have her company over the holidays are making sarcastic remarks. There is tension in the house.

It is filthy cold on the observation deck, but the lounge is so crowded and noisy with vacationing families that I cannot tolerate it. It is hard too to talk to each other; the noise of jet engines is almost unbearable. Even our parting kiss is destroyed by the cold wind and her worrying that there might be some one in the lounge who will report back to her parents. I am angry at her; she is old enough now to go her own way.

Once in my seat, I wave disconsolately. I don't care anymore. The whole thing has been too much of a strain.

EASTER: WILL THE BEASTS SUSTAIN US?

TEN DAYS AGO, along with the letter agreeing to spend the week together, she sent the manuscript. I could barely stand to read it, I was so angry. It was sentimental, full of misconceptions. It reduced the beast to something trivial. I started to write my comments, but was interrupted by too many meetings. I dropped some of my own work so I could send it to her before she came, but I was too late, so I took it with me to our rendezvous.

It was no use. She was full of the good news. It was going to be published, and she had already been paid well for it. A good friend was doing the illustrations. She showed me the galley proofs. Her friend's illustrations bore no resemblance to the classical unicorn. But that was to be expected; her story, after all, was the same.

She read the comments I had made on the manuscript one night after dinner. She was furious, waved the papers, shouted at me, and finally, when I refused to recant she stormed off to the spare room. She slept curled into a tight ball like a small hibernating animal. At breakfast she was sullen and withdrawn in spite of everything I did.

I went to the village for groceries in the afternoon and she was gone when I got back. She had taken both the original manuscript and the galley proofs.

I tried to feel sad that it was over, but couldn't because I was so terribly disappointed in her. Besides, the annual convention was much on my mind, and I absorbed myself in drawing up an agenda. The exchange of views between Richard and myself led to heated discussion in the past months, and the topic — *Will the Beasts Sustain Us?* — is to be the main one this year. I have to find a guest speaker, and it is important to find one who will not be partisan in any way. I draw up tentative lists, write letters, track down volunteers, work on an agenda.

MAY FIFTH

AND I MUST PREPARE my side of the debate, must defend the beasts against Richard (who is erudition and knowledge) as well as against Anne, (who is sentimentality), must maintain the delicate balance.

Quarantine

George McWhirter

THIS TIME IT IS twilight on a reafforested island. Inside the cabin a fire is burning, and inside the fire — a man. The fire, my reflection from the fireplace, grazes on the darkened belly of the room like a tapeworm; only an end of the woodpile will put a stop to these particular ruminations. And the man? I forgot: he burns and he doesn't burn; his name is Fotlac. And who am I? I'm the genius of the fire: at times, this man's conscience; at other times, his body; but, in short (to save compiling locations), I exist wherever something burns or there is heat: under this woman's armpit, for example, as she carries a Coleman lamp across the room and sets it on the table.

'Fotlac,' says the woman.

He huddles, groans. What does he most resemble, this man I have adopted? A gargoyle or will o' the wisp? Perhaps neither. There's no mischief in him, no glint in the eye. Fear, perplexity — yes; but the only wisp to be seen is a tiny comma of blue flame that curls beneath him, and from time to time a nervous exclamation that stutters from his rectum.

Fotlac is full of wind. Naturally. Ever since his assumption into the fire, he has been unable to swallow a scrap of food; everything he eats — fish, meat, vegetables — chars in his mouth; everything except water which evaporates and coats his sinuses with the minerals water normally leaves in suspension. Thirst he has come to regard as a dirty habit, hunger also. But I disagree: for what am I, but a sleepless appetite.

And Fotlac is afraid. What frightens him? Silence. The silence that followed his name when the woman said Fotlac, then stopped. His nerves make him more flatulent than usual, almost glad of my quarantine. Commas, dots — a dash of escaping methane.

Would she dare to place her fingers in the fire? So far she has molested each of his sensibilities, all but dragged him from me by his private parts. Such a woman! Proportionally there is more energy in one pore of her hand than in many of the volcanic suppurations I could mention. Clearly, she is more my foster child than he. Then why, the reader asks, isn't she inside the fire? To which I reply: there is no need.

She unscrews the primer on the lamp and pumps until the metal rod gives a pneumatic kick as if in ejaculation. Enough pressure, she decides, then performs as directed on the label: presses down on the top, spins the lock, twists the wire to clear the wick. Has his shrivelled beyond retrieving?

She crosses the room in the direction of the fire. On the way she remembers her father stripping emerald paint from the kitchen door door, his blow torch with its jet of violet flame buzzing round the nozzle, her mother singing:

> 'Busy, busy bee,
> I love the way you drip
> Bright honey down my hive.'

What honey has Fotlac manufactured? My heat plays upon her body like a memory.

Taking a taper from the mantelpiece, she pokes it into his nostril. The flames scuffling in and around it fly together as do his senses, alighting on the taper's end.

'What are you doing, Clodagh?' asks Fotlac.

'Can't you see? Lighting the lamp.'

When it's lit, she tosses the withered taper between his legs and looks away: an after image of the lamp hangs like strange albino fruit in the window; beyond it she begins to perceive the signs of plenty: huckleberries, oregon grape growing on charred stumps around the cabin.

Dare you do it?

Yes, I say. Take a firm grip the way you would on a nettle; my flame won't sting. But she doesn't recognize my voice, she thinks it is her own.

'Fotlac . . .' says Clodagh for the second time, setting the Coleman lamp on the mantelpiece with a rattle.

'Fotlac . . .'

'Clodagh, please . . .' answers the man inside me while his voice rises through the heatalator, disembodied, ventriloquized.

'If you had any love for me at all,' Clodagh goes on, 'you wouldn't have done it.'

'Clodagh, don't make things hard for me.'

'Hard,' replies Clodagh, her face drawn, the blue irises standing out from the whites of her eyes like the burners on a stove. She has given him the heat of her body, all of it for nothing.

'Hard!' she shouts, her voice shrill as a falcon's. 'What do you call hard? I come home at night and what do I find? You, barbecuing yourself. The only thing that isn't hard in this whole affair is your cock.'

'Clodagh . . .' A panicking voice passes out of the heatalator, over her head, wheezing like a sparrow's round the rafters. 'You don't understand. This is a stigma, a stigma.'

She's angry and so am I. As the rush of his breath hits me, I flare up in his teeth.

'Stigma,' Clodagh echoes him. 'Why didn't you stick yourself in me instead of the fire. It looks like I'm the one with the stigma.'

'In the name of Christ, Clodagh, don't be so foul mouthed. Try to understand.'

'Try? I have tried: I've understood,' says Clodagh. 'Didn't I understand when I raked the hard baked shit from under you. Thank God, you don't excrete any more, that's all I can say.'

'Clodagh, you're deliberately persecuting me.'

'You'll have plenty of that, Fotlac. Plenty. The wood supply's almost out,' she adds, 'we're down to the cedar you cut for kindling.'

'No.' The word bobs in the current of air coming through the heatalator. 'No, that can't be.'

'Yes, one cord of cedar — that's all.'

One cord of cedar . . . You could almost feel sorry for him, couldn't you. Clodagh? That terrible crackling, those explosions: each spark flying through the air sharp as a new thorn. But has he ever thought anything of you, I whisper; you, the woman he married.

'Fotlac, don't you feel anything at all?' she enquires.

The question fades on her lips and tears of frustration leak from the corners of her eyes.

Fotlac falls silent, and with tenderness, mistaking the source of those tears, he attempts to console her: 'Clodagh, you mustn't worry. I've told you: it's no worse than taking a bath; the sparks are like bubbles. It's not the cedar I'm afraid of really.'

'Bubbles, farts in the bath,' explodes his wife, 'that's not what I meant. I meant don't you feel anything for me?' She plucks up the hem of her nightdress, pulling it over her belly and up to her nose. 'If you loved me at all, you'd make it burn.'

I feel his eyes flickering this way and that in an attempt to avoid catching like two sparks in the tangle of hair.

'What do you mean — burn?'

'Have your brains dried up altogether. My bush, my empty nest. Make that burn, you hard-baked, puritanical turd.'

She pauses. Embarrassed and horrified, Fotlac buries his eyes in my ashes.

What can you do to get through to him, Clodagh? Perhaps if you took the bellows to him. I encourage her, but she reneges. To date huffing and puffing have got her nowhere, she concludes. I agree. Gently, gently does it.

'Fotlac, if you say it's like a bath, I want to share it. It could be a second honeymoon, a new beginning.'

'Clodagh,' stammers Fotlac, 'I said that to comfort you. But don't . . . It's terrible in here. You might burn. In the name of all that's holy behave like a Christian.'

'I am behaving like a Christian. I'm ready to burn . . . at the stake, if necessary.'

'Have patience, Clodagh.'

'I've had too much already.'

Far too much already.

'You must be enjoying yourself in there, otherwise you'd get out.'

Stake, sticks, the end of the woodpile. Like a bath . . . it's true, but, Fotlac, why did you tell her that. As he leaves a sigh, I crackle again in venemous response and my surge of extra heat makes him more uneasy. Wood: one cord of cedar chopped into fine sticks . . . all that's left.

'Clodagh, stop and think. Once you're in here, who'll feed the fire?'

Screwing up the front of her nightshirt into a ball, she stuffs it into her mouth as a gag to prevent herself from screaming.

'Without wood . . .' Fotlac hesitates, 'there's no guarantee the fire won't turn on us, devour us. Be sensible. Try burning a few sticks at a time. Clodagh, make what's left last out for my sake.'

Last out. Until what? Your cremation, Fotlac, or the slow, cold rigormortis after the fire has gone out. To die twitching like a goldfish in an empty tank, unredeemed, unredeemable. Do you remember reading of the dump outside Jerusalem? How those fires must have burned deep into the minds of the prophets: tapeworms of flame, thriving on the filth and the darkness. Are you in hell, my reverend Fotlac? Then, why don't you burn?

Clodagh unstops her mouth.

'Last,' she reiterates. 'I've lasted out too long. Much too long.

Either you come out or I come in. I warn you. I'll stoke no more fires, rake no more ashes from under that smoking arse of yours. What'll you do if the fire chokes?'

My very thought. Can you do without me, Fotlac?

'Clodagh, please listen to me. I never wanted any of this to happen.'

At this, she pulls up her nightgown and secretes two fingers in her private parts. Fotlac lowers his eyes. He places his head between his hands; these are the sides of the press from which he will squeeze the memory drop by drop: the wine, the blood, the fatal juice of their love and watch it fall into the ashes.

The pressure builds. Clodagh puffs and wheezes, coaxing from her body distant memories, nights on her back in the open field, night vegetable and carnal, and herself half flower, half beast, flourishing. In Fotlac's head as the memories take shape, peat briquettes, squares of turf tumble into a pile before his eyes.

THE DEVIL OR THE MOON: either could have been responsible. It was shortly after Evensong, and he was pedalling down the hill before coming to the bog. He often went there to be alone in the emptiness with only the *ignis fatuus* to keep him company. Something fluttered in the draft as he went by the gate that led to Cassidy's cottage. It was Clodagh, or rather, her skirt. He came back. There had been an odd glimmer, a liquid quality, full and dark, as if the lamp of his bicycle had struck two pools of dark oily water. Clodagh was naked from the waist up.

It wasn't as if such things were unheard of in lonely parishes. He remembered the incident in *Portrait of an Artist*, but this was no comfort: Clodagh was far from pregnant, her eyes gleamed at him like the temptress in the painting by Rousseau.

Why did allusions fog his mind? Perhaps he didn't want to think. He had intended to talk reason to her. But his mind kept groping for precedents; there was no precedent for what he did, or there were too many. No, it wasn't there: on a heap of turf at the rear of the cottage where Clodagh's flesh seemed to melt away and she smelt of something very deep and hot. I whispered fire between their legs.

A squawking startled them. Cassidy came out of the door in his unlaced boots, swinging the bucket. He was coming to get turf for the fire that burned winter and summer. The bucket gave off like a crow that had been startled in the trees, and Cassidy came to a halt.

'Evening,' he said.

Fotlac picked up a sod, more to hide his nakedness than to defend himself.

'Yes,' said Fotlac.

Her father looked at the bucket in his hand, then at Clodagh.

'Get your clothes on — you'll catch your death of cold standing there like that.'

'Aren't you going to say something?' Fotlac asked as Cassidy turned away. Words had to pass between them, words would bring relief.

'I expect you'll do your duty, Sir.'

He did. They were married on the day of St. Stephen, the first Christian martyr. Through me an obscene passion developed in Fotlac. He wanted to make all that was cold warm. Perhaps it was to salve his conscience by making everything an accomplice and demonstrating that everything could be kindled as he was, that the cold white marble of the altar could burn like magnesium or simple flesh, erupt as hard nubs of coal can into flame.

Clodagh chafed, but enjoyed it. Yet the altar never warmed: in the light of the candles he could see its whiteness glare at him like the cold flesh of the dead Christ. No, the flame which was in him was not to be, not yet; and not by his own will, but mine.

In his heart of hearts he had feared a sensual wife. He had wanted something beautiful which he could deny himself for the more pressing obligations of his ministry; something to which he could forever say goodbye, reminding himself that in the midst of life he was in death. It was his ministry he was to lose, not his life. He did not possess the kind of flower which would close on his going out and reopen again with gratitude on his return. A bog flower such as Clodagh Cassidy, plucked out of doors and emprisoned in a vase, can only foul the room; an odure of rot and regeneration creeps from her roots into the stamen and is exhuded through the fleshy labia of the petals.

WHEN SHE CATCHES his eye, Clodagh allows her fingers free play, growing in the process more flushed and furious.

'Clodagh, for God's sake, stop conducting yourself like an animal.'

Quitting this labour which has ceased to shock and merely becomes an act of self-abuse, she pulls the flowered nightdress over her head for one last attempt. She rolls it into a posy and offers it to him.

'Grill me from top to bottom if you want, but, for Christ's sake, do something.'

'Oh God.'

His eyes fall upon my ashes, but they remain bland and expressionless as the face of the almighty.

Clodagh catches his murmurings magnified in the heatalator. She remembers her father singing a song from the First World War:

'Twas on the day of the Armistice
Those Frenchies bared
Their fatted calves
And waved bunches of tiger lilies,
But we were thick with piss
And putrefaction.'

Piss and putrefaction: by his own admission this is what he amounts to. What's wrong with her? Who could make love to a man when he unloads his body on you like a piece of miserable excrement.

Without another word she turns on her heels and begins pulling the nightgown back over her head.

'Fotlac, you stink.' Her voice passes through the garment, muffled by the thickness of the cotton. 'You stink worse than burning camel dung.'

Still with arms and head trussed up in this floral sheaf, she begins to walk and blunders into the scuttle at the other end of the hearth, toppling sideways, and finally gouging her armpit on the corner of the hearth.

'Clodagh!'

Her name spills into the current of air rising steadily out of the heatalator.

But Clodagh doesn't hear because she has entered a swoon, spinning round like a hanged man cut loose from the gibbet. As her body sweeps down those last few inches, it fans the ashes into the air. They catch Fotlac in the teeth and her head thumps the hearth like a block of sodden wood.

Is she dead? There is no way he can test her pulse to see. Sap chirrups from the log beneath him, a cricket skitters across her face and he glares like a dazed bird from his perch following a spark as it worms its way along a few strands of Clodagh's hair

57

which lie sprayed across some embers. A living fuse.

He daren't breathe or move for fear the draft will set fire to her head. And in the event that she goes up . . . in that event, is he to blame?

FOR MONTHS AFTER they came to live on the island she pestered him, sunbathing . . . at every opportunity, exposing her breasts until they turned brown . . . brown, he told himself, as two heaps of turf. Human breasts capable only of sustaining the briefest of fires. And each night he took his bath boiling hot so that he could enter their bed and curl up, semi-cooked, like a prawn with the armour of his back held against her.

She enquired what was wrong: had he been playing with himself in the bath? After that, he lingered longer and longer in front of the fire before turning in. And his body . . . how heavy, awkward and unsightly it felt when saturated with water. It was a multiple hump he had to bear with him everywhere. Oh, to be light as ashes. What could transform him? Only me.

He bared his sexual equipment and stout pillars of his body to my blast, bringing his parts within a hairsbreadth of destruction. They grew measled, webbed like pink marble. Someone (his mother it must have been) told him that this tracery, these patterns were the maps the flames of hell would follow.

Would he burn? Not quickly enough. Had he always been burning with the fever of his body and always mortally cold inside. He introduced his foot to the fire. His toes, which should have been cooked like sausages, remained . . . still toes.

'Darling,' Clodagh called from the bedroom. 'Everything warm, ready and waiting. If you still think it's cold, I'll let you put your feet inside my nightshirt.'

Hearing no reply she came to investigate. Naturally, it took some time for him to convince her that he wasn't engaged in a process of self-cremation.

'There's nothing to be afraid of,' said Fotlac, 'I'm not melting like a candle, am I? I'm not burning in the normal sense.'

'No,' she observed.

'I haven't changed shape, swollen, blistered — anything like that?'

Looking at him more closely, she could perceive only two alterations: his complexion was blotched, a piebald fire roamed across his body, while the flames cresting on top of his skull concealed for a moment the fact that he was bald.

'Bald and in the buff,' she laughed; for the nightgown had

burnt off too. Then, she prodded him with the poker just to make sure that he was real.

THE LOG ON WHICH he is sitting gives way. His heel skids on the smooth ash and his foot prods Clodagh in the head. She ignites.

Hoary with ash and flame Fotlac crawls to her aid; at first on all fours, circling next baboonwise (he's still, well-nigh crippled after the long confinement), then there is a roar and he cranes his neck to watch the flames fly round the room. The door to an aviary seems to have opened; some flames become wild birds, some rosy coloured bats which hang upside down from the ceiling, some paroqueets which cackle, flapping their wings as they take flight from the wooden mantelpiece; many get tangled in the curtains.

One way or another he must get her from the room. But when he raises her body, it is only to brand it with the shape of his own. Yet still clutching her to him, he hobbles toward the door which opens like a new page on my story.

HOW LONG had he spent cloistered in the fireplace, studying, pondering a great mystery. Over and over he turned my flames: journals, textbooks, liturgies; flame, enflamed and flame again; but this single act — the incineration of his wife — has, with one fell swoop, shown him the significance of all his thought and action, his passion to abrade and obliterate the body. His intransigence was the flintstone against which his wife was to grind her body, and from which would spring my fire, all be it, unquenchable. The act — his whole life — seems anarchic. I came to roost in him. I ground my talons in his bowels. In the name of God he had tried to destroy so that something would rise again; he carries the burden of that resurrection in his arms.

Strange, he says this twice inwardly before he can digest it. The door flaps behind wafting blue grey smoke into the air. Clodagh doesn't burn. Like a log of compressed paper steeped in kerosene, the flames feed on the released gasses and leave a corona of fire around her body. She sleeps in my golden cocoon. Toward what honeymoons, what new consummations are they moving?

Birds, insects, animals take flight, and a galaxy of sparks whirls around the topmost branches of the firs: smell of a huge beast in dry, unbearable rut. He loses his bearings, he and I fanned by the wind. He runs in a semi-crouch, sometimes dragging her, sometimes bearing her in a fireman's lift, always forg-

ing on until his legs turn to jelly or pure fire as he tries to outstrip himself; but, whicheverway he turns, there are trees, trees and more trees.

Why did he run inland? Behind the house lay twenty miles of lakefront. He stares at me. I leap-frog from tree to tree. Monkey, baboon of flame, biting, chittering, scratching. I preen, fascinated bird, rollicking; fierce feathers plumed in the beginning by the sun.

Treacherous, more treacherous than the will o' the wisp which lures one soul at a time, I will sweep across the island gathering people to my body the way snowballs gather snow. Who will separate us?

He switches direction, first tacking right, then left. With a clattering of many wings the wind carries my bright plague toward the East and the town of Port Alberni.

Measures are taken against me. A firecrew throws up a firebreak somewhere between my body and the town. There will be water-bombers to sap my strength; after that they will attack from both flanks and eventually, hopefully, put me out.

Before the beaters are allowed to close in, the bombers make their run, flying low, releasing their eggs which split in mid air, and fall, exploding and hissing all around Fotlac.

What was bright in me is now blackened. He stumbles forward, three quarters extinguished, and Clodagh rolls over and over, her breasts, buttocks and rounded parts becoming balls of fire, and the earth onto which she falls quickens and flares. The remnants of my fire that cling to Fotlac's thighs and abdomen are rewoven.

She gets up. What is she doing? Twisting and twining, every sinew of her body illuminated as she rubs her back against the trees. He watches the violet flame purring from her open mouth. What noxious gas — methane? She must be put out before she makes an exhibition of herself.

When news arrives of how the bombers first run has failed, the Fire Chief orders another. Impossible, he is told, impossible. Too little time to refuel and refill the tanks. Some other measure must be taken.

'Piss!' the Fire Chief spits into the microphone and glances out the window of his staff car. 'Why doesn't it rain?'

'Send more trucks up No. 1 Road,' he roars at his waiting lieutenant, 'that will get them in close.'

'Will the bombers be ready in another hour?' he asks H.Q.. 'The first will have reached the break by then.'

'Yes,' comes the reply.

'Fine.'

He snaps off the machine and replaces the microphone.

One hour later I crest on the firebreak. Fotlac struggles against the undertow. Where is she? He can't find her anywhere. Then snatches of a song can be heard drifting between the bellows of the fire.

'I just want to set your trunks on f-o-i-r-e.'

Bawdbeautiful she comes in sight, cat with golden hackles who slinks along the line of the firebreak, singing off key, brokenly, with consumate delight. Fotlac plops his bottom on a stump. Thoughts . . . what becomes of them?

Enlightenment, crude fire?

He rises, wipes his hand across his forehead, then he weaves right, left. I watch each move; the cat with golden hackles stalks; we meet, for the first time sensing a proper pain, her nails in his back shredding the years' neglect. I inflate his groin.

He pumps and pumps. She will not go out, he cannot, and — for once — I do. They billow soft as napalm as it should be. As the bombers unload, Fotlac sees that none of us are made of the darkness where we dream. We see because we issue light. I am as simple as touch, even in the wet, the cold wet skin of the raincoast, I touch off.

Entropy

Eugene McNamara

A POCKET PULLED inside out. Theory of black hole. A star winks out like a shut eye which never opens again. In 1842, Sadi Carnot developed notion that available energy must be degraded in time. This theory refined 1850 by R. Clausius. Energy degraded through work into a form that can no longer be used. Therefore, as process goes on and on, it takes more and more and more energy to get, in return, less and less and less.

This process is depressing.

1959. It was the year when everyone he knew was reading *The Alexandria Quartet*. There were a lot of discussions about it. It gave a certain ironic focus to their lives. They all agreed that they lived at the end of the stupidest decade in all of history. See Spengler. They felt sorry for themselves. They were very ironic.

They were excessively literary. There was a girl in this group who thought that she looked like Clea in the *Quartet*. De Witt Lawrence thought so too. She also thought that she looked like Peyton Loftus in *Lie Down in Darkness*. He thought so too. Because of his sensitivity to these resemblances, she admired him. Now. Who did *he* look like? He feared that it was the constipated Englishman in the *Quartet*.

Ah, literature. Literature and romance. Literature and sex. In those days one did not just go to bed. It had to have significance. One did it to classical music.

'It's somehow, I don't know,' the girl who looked like Clea/-Peyton (Her name was what? Her mother was Jewish and romantic. Naomi?) 'It's somehow so sordid.'

'Yes,' he said. His name was De Witt. It was a family name. He had hated it for twenty some years. Then he became fond of it. It implied breeding and elegance, two qualities he feared he did not have.

'Yes,' he went on, 'but that cello music in the background — sounds baroque — turns the sordid into dalliance —'

It was May in 1959 and the station on the radio in her apartment was playing Vivaldi.

'You know,' he said afterwards, 'it's at times like these — like this — when I feel, I don't know, when I fear — or doubt — my own existence. I'm sort of like an empty pocket. You could pull it inside out and then where would I be. I wouldn't be there at all —'

'Sad,' she said sleepily, 'post coitum or something triste —'

Twenty years later in May he would remember the Vivaldi and Durrell and the girl, in that descending order. For the life of him, twenty years later, he could not think of conjure up rack his brain as he might, sitting at his desk twenty years later down the road in the credit office of the hotel chain he worked for, whose main office was on the top floor of the chain's original establishment, built in flush 1928, lots of Aztec inspired ornamentation, brass elevator doors, new paint on the walls and high ceilings, new carpeting in halls, reading: credit must not be extended anymore to Clayton Holmes of Atlanta, Georgia, had run up astounding tab in his native state, in New Orleans, Chicago, Montreal and San Francisco, and airplanes in between and paid nothing, zip, diddley, this notice to be sent to all hotels in chain, and he pictured Clayton Holmes looking like Scobie in *Quartet*, or rumpled white suit Tennessee Williams or with seignorial face of Bernini Cardinal, shrewd, sensual, subtly brutal, imagine Clayton when he learns of credit cut off, smashing hapless head of desk clerk in Atlanta New Orleans Chicago with a silver wolfshead handled walking stick, her face, her face, her voice saying *sad*.

Name. He remembered where she lived back in 1959. What the room they lay in looked like. She had been a year younger than he. Bothered her. She wanted lover in thirties or forties who would be tender and sad, someone in the movies they went to in theatre where they served coffee in lobby and stood around talking about movies which they called cinema, and she had a job as lab technician for an industrial outfit, he had often thought of her wearing one of those white lab coats, sitting on a high stool at a zinc countered bench, looking at test tubes, marking things down on a clip board, distracted, pushing a damp tendril, it would be summer and warm, of hair off her cheek with a pencil, yellow, hair what colour, her name was Alicia.

Alicia. Now each Friday after work he met Colin and they had a drink or two. They were the last of the crowd who used to be so literary and ironic. He and Colin worked for same hotel chain though on different floors of the building and seldom saw one another except on Fridays. They lived in different suburbs and were each married to different women and sometimes both were invited to the same party given by mutual friends. Both had grown children, watched television, and did not read serious books anymore or go to theatres where they called the movies cinema. He and Colin had little to say to one another. Even on Friday afternoons.

They sat at the bar, ate the peanuts from the little bowls, De Witt surreptitiously licking the salt from his fingers, he hated the way he smeared his glass, sudden remembering one of his children's glasses peanut butter smeared back when? when? who? and he and Colin drank and said little and looked around the bar.

L'Automne, the voice on the radio had said in her room on that May morning, *L'Allegro initial est une danse rustique* —

'I saw Albert last night,' Colin said, pronouncing it Al bare. 'He was out West someplace.'

Al bare, also from the ironic group, was now a television commentator. He was often on the National. You could tell where he was from the background. These were establishing shots. If it was a picturesque fishing village over his shoulder it was the Maritimes. If it was a grain silo, the Prairies. A refinery meant Alberta.

'Was he in front of a grain elevator or a refinery?' said De Witt.

'I think it was a totem pole,' said Colin tossing peanuts into his mouth from a loosely clenched fist. 'Means Vancouver.'

'No. Vancouver would be a lot of ships anchored and unmoving and not being loaded or unloaded,' said De Witt, signaling and not being seen by the bartender, was he for godssake invisible the uppity bastard swine like to kick his face in.

'Anyway,' said Colin. Colin had lost a lot of hair in past twenty years and gotten, well, not fat, just thick all over, larger, took up more space. 'He looked good. Hasn't changed.'

'Everybody on TV looks good,' said De Witt, looking up and then down and then away from the back of a woman squeezing her way between the people at the bar and the tables, not much room, coats hanging over the backs of the bar stools and over the backs of the chairs at the tables making a thick skin of coat to rub impersonally no malice the sides of anyone trying the gauntlet necessary the washrooms were back there she looked familiar the back of her neck there she half turned.

'Don't envy his success,' said Colin. 'I really don't.'

'Listen,' said De Witt. 'Do you remember a girl named Alicia? I brought her to Hillary's party? New Year's?'

'No,' said Colin, then smiling with delight, 'Yes! Yes! The one with the nice bum. Chemist or something. Or did she marry a chemist?'

'Neither. But I wondered —'

'Alicia,' marveled Colin, signaling to the bartender who did not see him either minor satisfaction, 'Have you seen her lately?'

'No,' said De Witt, waving more vigorously and the bartender finally thank god saw and De Witt signaled two more. 'But I was wondering if you maybe remembered her last name? I've been trying to remember it all damn day. Was it Clifton? Clinton? Clanton? Began with a "c" or a *cluh* sound —'

'I thought it was something like "к"' said Colin. 'Here, let me. My round. Keegan? Kelly? Kelsey? Kingsley — no, Kimball — Kirkwood! That's it! Alicia Kirkwood! Uh huh, uh huh!'

'No,' said De Witt. 'Thanks. This one will have to be my last. Have to get home about sixish. No, wasn't Kirkwood — But that's *close*, that's *close* —'

It wasn't close. Ten years earlier he and Colin had gone for lunch and Colin had confessed carrying on, having an affair not just a fling, it was serious and here he was, poor Colin, married seventeen? no eighteen years and the girl my god! hardly older than his own daughter.

'It's a cartoon situation,' De Witt had said back then. 'It's in the movies and the novels and all over. I think I saw it on TV last week. Col, this is a joke situation.'

'I know. I am a character in a cartoon,' said Colin. 'I always have been. Only now I accept my cartoonhood.'

After lunch, De Witt thought *I* am living in a cartoon. Why is everything so banal. He himself had gone through Colin's so predictable crisis less than a year ago and he had not burdened Colin with it. Did that give him a slight moral edge?

Ten years later, after the lunch, leaving Colin at the bar, TGIF Happy Hour prices over, Colin staying for one more though, De Witt remembered Colin's divorce, no, not over that girl, later one, name also not remembered, from whom now also divorced, living alone, jealous of Al bare's success. It wasn't Kirk-wood. He took the subway, then the bus, a commuter in Cheever Updike Kirkwood no definitely a *cluh* sound.

He had left Colin back at the bar having a last drink. He never saw Colin again.

On Monday morning, he fed Alicia Kirkwood, Clanton, Clifton, Clanton, Clinton, Casey, Clancy, Jewish mother, true, but possible Irish father into the computer and nothing came up. Well, of course by now perhaps certainly married widowed divorced remarried using maiden name or maiden name dash married name dead.

He gave the computer Alicia's age last known address date of graduation high school university computer told him could not compute inadeq info in its green tinted light as if a voice from the bottom of a pool in the sea.

He remembered now that they had not exactly parted on good terms. It had been his fault. He had acted badly. He had hurt her. He had left her flat. He had behaved caddishly.

And twenty years. Why would she want to see him after all that time. She happily married living in suburb exurb fancy tarted up old slum area now sandblasted interiors gutted husband a huge success large powerful man handsome all his hair jogger karate expert could make her come and moan orgasms every day and night often takes her on vacations they swim in blue blue waters De Witt sees only on Surftours brochures for godssake why would she want to see De Witt.

De Witt feared being pistol whipped.

De Witt feared being pistol whipped beaten with chains shot stabbed slashed kicked in the balls choked prick out off burned with lighted cigarettes bashed on head drenched with boiling water in a coma buried alive cancer rotting hell heaven derision can't get it up out of work old old and feeble looking foolish vanishing not existing anymore

At lunch ten years ago, he and Colin had shared a small pizza and green salad and had house wine. They had split the bill. The place was trendy, Colin said. Today Colin would say it was high tech. No anchovies on the pizza. No onions in the salad

67

please, we have to go back to work, waitress smiles. Had heartburn all afternoon. Dumb to have pizza for lunch. Sleepy all afternoon. Gas on stomach. Surreptitious fart.

All this De Witt remembered. Alicia *cluh*. Zero.

Perhaps Alicia married to Clayton Holmes. Now credit cut off no more high life all those cities would she leave him now, now that he's broke, Alicia in a slip lying on bed in broken down joint, Alicia Holmes, neé cluh. Ceiling fan turns slowly.

Second Law of Thermodynamics takes effect. See papers R. Clausius 1850, 1852.

De Witt liked to read the Mafiosi novels. They gave him a sense of family. He liked the cop shows on tv. Gave him sense of order. Liked to read Nazi war criminals conspiracy secret society ex s.s. Satisfied growing sense of paranoia. Did not read occult possession novels. They only contributed to growing sense of powerlessness before unseen forces. Did not read sex novels. Reasons obvious.

'I'm expensive,' said the fat man. 'Twenty-five a day and expenses.'

Afternoon light fell with difficulty through the grime on the window, lighting up the letters De Witt read backwards semloH, etavirP and dimly fell on the fat man's white suit.

'It's worth it to me,' said De Witt. 'Here's fifty as a retainer.'

'So many people missing,' the fat man sighed, clawing up the money and turning to look out or at the window, 'and so many lovers wanting to find them —'

As De Witt came down in the wrought iron cage elevator he saw a woman in a black raincoat and beret going up the stairs to the detective's office? and caught a glimpse of the side of her face as his car went down and she went up the stairs and for just the pause of a breath he thought —

'All right bud,' says the detective in a weary voice, rubbing the backs of his fingers into his eyes, leaning back in the swivel chair so it creaked, 'Why all this sudden interest in this Alicia, huh? Maybe you did away with her back in, when, 1959, or so and all this sudden *concern* is to throw suspicion someplace else.'

The detective gets up, De Witt's stomach tenses pistol whipped clubbed kidneys third degree no bruises the good guy bad guy routine it will hurt to pee.

'Here in these files,' says the detective, opening and closing a file drawer, flipping a hand over the folders, 'we have every conceivable kind of crime. Break and enter with intent. Common assault. We even have *un*common assault. Guy buggered a turkey. We had the turkey in here as evidence. Turkey shit everywhere. Anyhow, murder, arson, rape, you name it. Somewhere in all this there may be an unsolved file on a lady. Lady named Alicia. And you claim there's nobody who can remember her last name.'

Well, thought De Witt, that isn't *quite* true. If truth be known, his wife Jean probably remembered it. He had met Jean right after breaking with Alicia and Jean hadn't been overly fond of the group he hung with, poseurs she called them, and Colin, dear friend, kindly told her of his long long liaison with Alicia. Jean had never met Alicia. But she probably remembered the last name. She would. But the ironic thing was that she was the one person in the world that he couldn't wouldn't never ever ask.

'Arrest him, Lieutenant,' says Clayton Holmes in a waspish voice, 'Or let me hit him with my walking stick —'

'Get out of my office, you fruit,' says the detective in his weary voice. 'I'll get to you in a minute.'

'OK, Lawrence, you can go now. We can't hold you. Yet. But don't leave town. Don't play detective,' says the weary voice. 'Don't be cute. Let us do our job. We're good at it.'

Closeup of detective's face. Grainy skin. Few pockmarks. Evidence of harsh street urban childhood. Eyes that have seen everything. Buggered turkeys. Dismembered corpses. Eyes you can't fool. De Witt's twenty years working for same firm twenty years married same woman no convictions children never in trouble no drug busts not even a speeding ticket but all the same De Witt felt guilt guilt guilt as those eyes looked at him fade to black.

Reinstate credit Clayton Holmes 2798L0056 MT he typed into the computer. Authority D. Lawrence. Override previous memo. After all, he thought, why should *she* suffer?

'You should have come to me,' Jean said in a sad but gentle voice. Evening was coming on. They hadn't turned the kitchen light on yet.

'I should have known,' Jean went on. 'Back then you used to slip sometimes and call me Alicia and I wondered how you knew —'

'Knew,' said De Witt in a foolish guilty shamed voice.

'That I was Alicia,' said Jean. 'Oh Dee it was *delicious* to fool you all that time.'

Then she laughed. It was now so dark in the breakfast nook that he could not see her face. Was she smiling? Had she removed a mask and revealed the hidden face? Was all this a cruel joke? Had Colin —

'Let's have some light,' he said in a manly voice, reaching for the rheostat.

Hands gripped his arms neck left thigh in brutal pinching obviously expert style. He could not move.

'No,' came her cool voice. 'Let's not have light. Not yet. You may release him now. He won't be troublesome.'

The hands obeyed instantly, as if snapping to attention.

'That about wraps it up man,' said the weary detective with the knowing eyes. He flipped his little notebook shut and pushed it into an inside pocket.

'People all over are vanishing without a trace,' he said as he got up from the couch with an effort the cushions tended to sag in the middle.

Alicia looked pale beautiful and composed wearing simple little nothing black dress. She nodded bravely.

'We'll keep in touch,' said the detective. 'And here's my card if you hear anything. I mean *anything*. I can be reached any time day or night.'

As he went down the walk towards the unmarked car at the curb, Alicia watched him. Clayton came out of the kitchen with two large glasses. The ice in the glasses made a duh duh sound against the sides.

'Can I come out now? Not too early for these, is it lover?' he said in a suave tone.

'Never too early,' said Jean, 'Or too late, for that matter.'

Her voice, he thought, like rubbed silk, eyes smoky and dangerous. She reached for her glass and her fingers brushed just for an instant Clayton's fingers curved around the glass beads of moisture forming on the glass he felt twinge of fear.

'When you go in tomorrow,' she said in the voice all had to obey, 'erase him from the computer's memory bank. Tomorrow. He must no longer exist.'

'He never did,' said Clayton in a reassuring tone. He had to stifle an impulse to crash the heels of his boots together as they raised their glasses. Tomorrow.

'I don't know what to say, Mrs. Lawrence,' said the weary detective. 'All this business about secret societies and people missing and conspiracies and fat private detectives in white suits. It's like a late movie or channel switching late at night. It was all a smoke screen for the truth.'

'Truth,' said Alicia in a resigned beautiful voice. 'Who knows what that is.'

'In the Department,' the detective said, 'we deal in facts. Not fiction. Nothing made up. Things in the files. Hard evidence. Trial exhibits numbered in sequence. Reality. It's sometimes not too pretty. But it's real.'

'Real,' said Jean in the same let's get this over with voice. 'Who knows what that is.'

'Let's skip all this French existentialist stuff,' said the detective. 'I think we'd better be getting downtown now.'

'Downtown. Who —'

'The driver knows the way,' said the detective, opening the door. 'Shall we go?'

'Kindness of strangers,' said

As they walked down towards the unmarked car, she could see the driver's arm on the opened window ledge. It was a fat arm. The white shirt sleeve had been opened, sleeve rolled back. Fat hairy arm on the opened window ledge of the car.

'What can I say, lady,' said the fat detective behind the wheel, 'So long it's been good to know you?'

'Shut up and drive,' said the weary detective.

'Drive he said,' the fat detective smiled back at them.

She could see herself in his sunglasses. She couldn't see the weary detective sitting next to her. If she looked only in the sunglasses, she saw two versions of herself, identical, side by side. Nobody existed except her and the images or rather only the images existed in her act of perceiving and when the fat driver turned his face away she would not exist anymore and then he

'Metro police called it one of most bizarre,' said the deep rich good voice from the TV, 'and here is Albert Soin with an update —'

Cutout figure in front of city hall, possessor of knowledge, certain knowledge.

Workpoints:
1. Clea and Clayton in Alexandria.
2. Clayton as El Scob.
3. De Witt on Greek island with Clea's child.
4. Background music. *The Four Seasons*.

Clifton Webb (1893-1966) in *Laura* and *Dark Corner*. Dana Andrews detective in *Laura*, Mark Stevens in *Dark Corner*. William Bendix (1906-1964) as hireling in *Dark Corner* in white suit

Inadeq

Inadeq info

does not compute

reprogram

end of series reprogram

1959. It was the year when Alicia met De Witt. The sex wasn't all that great but Alicia knew how to bide her time. She knew that she had a destiny. It was a destiny to be one of the most powerful women of her age.

his hot throbbing

her heaving

powerful brutal pressing crushing she

1959 it was

The Steps

Garry McKevitt

WE THOUGHT WE HAD SEEN IT EARLIER, but then it had only broken slightly through the surface of the water and we had decided that it was a fish jumping. But there was no mistaking now that it was a Killer Whale. It was just a few feet beneath the surface beside the boat and was very leisurely doing the same ten knots as we were.

Klaus, my customer, was fascinated by it. Leaning out on the railing, he shouted back to me over the inboard's noise: 'My God, it's huge. Is it dangerous?'

'Not at all,' I shouted back, 'they are badly named,' though I thought to myself that most seals and fish wouldn't agree with me, and it was difficult not to feel intimidated being this close to one in the wild. They were playful and cheerful doing tricks in an aquarium, but it was different here where my boat might become its plaything. Still, despite my slight nervousness, it was hard not to be overcome by the sleek beauty and size of the thing. It was almost the same length as my twenty-five foot fishing boat and obviously could equal any speed it was capable of.

The whale seemed to stay with us quite a long time though I imagine it was really only a few minutes. Then it left as quickly as it came: emerging up out of the water as if it wanted to have one final good look at us and then diving down and away from the boat and out of sight.

Klaus hurried back from the bow. 'What a wonderful creature,' he said, 'I thought it was a dolphin at first, but it was much bigger than that. Do you know anything about them?'

I racked my brain to think of what I knew about Killer Whales. I had always been interested in them but never enough to learn much about them. I remembered something I once read: 'The Indians around here used to think very highly of them at one time. They were a sacred animal.'

'Why?'

'It seems to me that they believed the Killer Whale was the reincarnation of their bravest fishermen. As you can imagine, it was a terrible thing to kill one.'

'What happened if you killed one?' Klaus shot back.

His intenseness put me slightly off balance and I couldn't remember right away. Slowly the answer came to me: 'They didn't get any more fish I guess. Yes, that was it. One of the ways they found fish was by going where the Killer Whales were. I guess they figured that if they killed one, they wouldn't only be killing one of their greatest ancestors, they would also lose one of their key methods of finding fish.'

'Don't you think,' Klaus said, 'it would have been a terribly brave thing for one of those fishermen to kill a whale?'

'No,' I said, 'I would think it would have been a very stupid thing to do, considering what they believed.'

'Yes, but what an act of heroism,' he motioned with his hand out over the water as if they were all around and he was lecturing to them in his own pseudo-dramatic way. 'What an act of heroism to burn all the bridges. To be the first one to, knowing full-well the consequences, perform the damnable deed.'

'If you, and everyone around you, lived on fish,' I said, 'it wouldn't seem too heroic.' I knew what he was getting at but I didn't feel like encouraging him.

He came down off his toes and looked at me and decided, I suppose, that he was wasting his breath on a hick fishing guide like myself. Instead of pursuing his theme, he turned and looked out over the bow and said, 'How soon will we be there?'

'We should almost be able to see them now,' I said. 'Yes, there! Just starboard of the bow.'

Klaus had hired me to take him to see a man-made oddity known locally as 'The Steps'. He said he'd heard about them from someone in Salish Bay (the place I worked out of) and was curious to see this strange artifact left by a countryman of his. 'The Steps' were, according to the local story, supposed to have been built around the turn of the century by a rich German immigrant, who had plans on building a house there to bring his fiancé to. That was the hitch in his plans, they said, for she didn't come and he gave up on his construction after getting this far, though some stories say that he did begin work on a house somewhere up in the hills.

As we looked at them Klaus urged me to tell him everything I knew about them. He thought they were quite interesting, and they were: there in the middle of nowhere, ascending in white concrete and granite up out of the water to the edge of the forest. They were like a jagged rip in the reality of the place, through which, if one knew the right incantations, one could enter into another world.

'When I was a kid,' I told him, 'I used to come out here with friends to camp. It was kind of a spooky place sometimes.'

'You mean because of the steps?'

'Well, we always had a feeling that the man who built them was somehow still around. You know how it is by a campfire at night. There's always that sound in the bush behind you that you can't explain. We were sure it was him coming to tell us to get off his land. We'd stare into the fire and dare each other to look behind. You see another version of the story has it that he never did leave. He was supposed to have gone nuts when his woman wouldn't come out and he ended up spending the rest of his life prowling around alone up in the hills above here.'

'But you really don't believe that's true anymore,' Klaus said, smiling at me.

'Well, you know, there's always a part of you that likes to believe those kinds of things and I don't really mind that,' I said.

'Yes, I suppose you're right,' Klaus said, 'but I never did think much of fairy tales.'

'Well, that's the legend,' I said, as I headed the boat back to Salish Bay.

After that trip I thought I had seen the last of Dr. Hans Klaus, but unfortunately I was wrong.

I was down in the bar of the Salish Bay Inn a couple of days later having a conversation with a scotch and water. The 'Anchorage' was one of those places lethargically decorated to appear 'nautical' with ropes and nets and cork floats suspended from the roof in a haphazard fashion. It was dark and generally empty, and so over the years I had given up even looking around the place when I drank there. What was the point? I was taken completely by surprise then, when Henry, the bartender, informed me that someone had bought me a drink. 'You've got the wrong person. In fact, you've got the wrong bar,' I said. But this was the only bar, and as it turned out there were only two people in it: Klaus and myself. He motioned me over to sit with him.

'Being from Germany, you obviously are not aware of the local customs,' I said. 'Nobody buys drinks for anyone around here. It's bad luck.'

'You seem to be an expert on bad luck, Mr. Clarke.'

'Yes, very good. Well . . . it's just one of my many interests.'

'I want to hire you again in two days,' he said. 'Will you be free?'

'I think so, sure,' I said. 'What do you want to do: more sightseeing, or some fishing this time?'

'I thought hunting.'

'Hunting? Well, I'm sorry, I can't really help you there. That's really not my line.'

'I want to go back out to The Steps, and I need a boat to get there.'

'That much I can do for you,' I said, 'but why The Steps? There're lots of places around here to hunt that you can get to without a boat.'

'Well I guess you were right the first time in a way. I want to do some sightseeing too.'

Klaus was silent for a moment. He shuffled uneasily in his chair and then said, 'The man who built that place was my grandfather. I'd just like to have a little look around and, maybe, if I got lucky, have a shot or two at a deer.'

He said it so nonchalantly that it took a moment for it to sink in, and then I found it hard to take him seriously, though he was completely serious. Nonetheless, I could find nothing to say and so Klaus continued: 'He was kind of a legend, as well, in our family. He disappeared long before I was born, so my knowledge of him is all second-hand.'

'Then this business about his fiancé and everything wasn't true. I mean, you said you were his grandchild.'

'Yes, actually it wasn't a fiancé. It was his wife and children who were supposed to follow him out. When he got here, it was he who didn't want them to come. I guess he liked his new freedom or something.' Klaus' voice had an edge on it. He picked up his cigarettes and pocketed them and started to get up from the table. 'That's about all I can tell you right now, Mr. Clarke.'

'Did he really spend the rest of his life in the woods out here?'

'It's a long story,' he said, as he rose to his feet, 'and I have a feeling, now, that I shouldn't have brought it up. It's something I've never really talked much about to anyone.'

'Well now's a good time to start,' I said.

'No, I'm sorry. Perhaps some other time. See you later,' he said, and, bobbing his head slightly to miss a cork float, he strode out of the bar.

* * *

BOTH KLAUS AND I thought it was a whale again when we first saw the movement a few hundred feet ahead of the boat. But as we got closer we soon realized it was a swimming deer: its head just arched up out of the water.

'There's an easy kill for you,' I said.

'Too easy,' he replied, 'I don't believe in shooting game out of its element.' He turned back to watch the deer. It had just reached shore and was over the rocks and into the forest in one quick, graceful movement. It reminded me of the way a fish takes to water when it escapes the net.

Once at the steps, Klaus was interested in taking a trail that led to a small creek about a mile back in the forest up the other side of a ridge. It had been years since I had been along it but it was still fairly clearly marked.

It was a difficult trail to follow at first, as the lower part was covered an inch deep in a fragmented parchment of arbutus leaves that caused us to continually slip back. Once inside the forest, the path broadened slightly and levelled out and footing became easier in the soft loam. Though the ridge was steep, the path hairpinned in such a way that one was not aware of the altitude one was gaining. Off to the side and behind us the forest gradually closed off the sea and, but for the swishing of our feet, the quiet became pervasive.

It came as somewhat of a surprise when we broke out into a small clearing at the top of the ridge and had a clear view down into the slash of the ravine and creek itself a hundred yards below us. Though the slope was as steep as that which we had just hiked, the creek had created a wide and flat base. It was the dry season and there was little water running, though still enough to fill out several wide pools at intervals along its path. The bed was a continuous sculpture of undulations and smooth curves of sandstone. Off to our left we could just make out a sliver of sea.

The trail joined the stream at the largest of these pools. Klaus, however, wanted to head upstream and started down the slope through light bush to the section of the stream directly below us. After a few splashes of its cool water over our faces we turned and headed upstream. The first few hundred yards we had some difficulty making our way along the slick and convoluted faces of the sandstone, but the going became easier as the stream flattened out and we had easy footing along the dry fine gravel at its edges. On both sides, the steep slopes of the narrow valley stretched up, hemming us in. The sun was high in the sky now and if it weren't for the coolness of the stream, our trek would have been tedious business. As it was, the constantly changing aspects of the stream and low grade of its descent made for a very pleasant hike. We walked single file, with Klaus in front, and we seldom spoke. Somehow, I didn't feel much like a guide. I wondered if this was part of the hunt or part of the sightseeing. It was over an hour later when my question was answered.

The ravine we had been walking up quite suddenly opened up into the pocket of a valley about a quarter of a mile across. Instead of following the creek bed, which now snaked away in front of us through thick deciduous foliage, Klaus stopped briefly, scanned very slowly the valley's breadth and then headed straight off at a sharp angle into the bush. The going was difficult. There had obviously been a fire here at one time, or perhaps logging, and although secondary growth was starting to dominate, the underbrush was extremely thick and snarled. We had to walk in a hunched position making our way head first, with the faith that the rest of our bodies would somehow clamber and slip and scrape over and through the twisted vines and salal, and follow along. It was a kind of controlled falling but as is the case in this kind of bush it is often the only way one can make any distance. I began to complain but Klaus impatiently waved back at me to be quiet. He was beginning to get on my nerves, but I continued to follow anyway. I noticed for the first time then that he had a compass out. He seemed very certain of where he was going. And, with the first sighting of a low concrete foundation just barely emerging like a Mayan ruin out of the jungle floor, I realized that one would need foreknowledge to find it. No one else would willfully trudge as far as we had into this entangled maze without a very definite reason and direction.

Klaus almost showed excitement as he stepped up on to the wall and turning, rested back against the bush and smiled at me. 'This is it, Mr. Clarke, the beginnings of my grandfather's house.'

'I thought we were looking for deer,' I said. For some reason I felt cheated. Perhaps I felt just then that childhood fantasies should be left alone.

'Well we are, in a way,' he said, 'but I just had to see this for sure. I just had to find out if everything was as it should be . . . and it is, it is — exactly.'

We started to make our way around the perimeter of the

foundation but it was very hard going. What we did see of it, trailing off into the bush, indicated that it was huge: a foundation of a house that would have been impressive in any setting. After a while Klaus stopped and, breaking a space in the vines with his heavy boots, removed his pack and rifle and sat down on the wall. I did the same and accepted with some pleasure the sausage and bread he began to deal out of the bag. It was well into the afternoon, and I was beginning to feel a little weak.

Klaus seemed in a very genial mood, the reticence of a few nights before had passed. 'You see, Mr. Clarke, once my grandfather got his supplies over the ridge, he used the summer river bed, which is easily wide enough to haul them up to this valley. He had explored the area well and decided that this was the most ideal spot. The wide fertile valley, when cleared, would have supplied more than his needs in garden produce as well as offering a perfect naturally enclosed pasture for cattle. And the stream would supply year round water . . .'

'Yes, I agree,' I said, 'but for a man of his wealth it hardly seems necessary to go to all this trouble. Would'nt it have been easier and more convenient to build down at the mouth of the stream by the sea? The climate is so mild all year round in this country that it would have been no problem bringing in his needs by boat from the village.'

'My grandfather was not looking for convenience or easiness. He would have stayed in Germany if those were his desires. No — he was a much more complex man than that, a very strange man in fact. Would you like to see a picture of him?'

I nodded. Klaus reached in his pack and after carefully laying out its contents on the top of the foundation, retrieved a small leather satchel from the bottom, out of which he pulled a postcard sized photograph. He handed it to me.

It was obviously a photograph of a photograph and though the age of the original and the process of reproduction had robbed it of some detail, it was not difficult to recognize the extreme likeness between this man and the man sitting beside me: the same close cropped hair, the same large roundish head and the same quiet coolness in the eyes. The photograph was of the head and upper body. He wore an officer's jacket and his overall demeanor was softened a certain amount by a full moustache. I looked at Klaus and then back at the photo; these were men who were certain of themselves and what they wanted.

I handed the photograph back. 'There's no mistaking that he's a relation of yours.'

Klaus gave me that strange half-smile of his, 'Yes. Well they say that I am very much like him in many ways, including appearance. He was a hunter too, you see.'

'Is that why he came out to this country?'

'Yes. I guess you could say that was the main reason. I suppose that was the main attraction. But once he got here things changed somewhat. You see, he discovered that quite by accident he had bought an ancient mystery, a legend along with the land. He wrote about it back to my father and I came upon the letters just a short while ago. It seems that the main labour force around here at that time was the local Indians. So, as it happened, he was to spend a fair amount of time with them. My grandfather was somewhat of an adventurer, Mr. Clarke, and through his travels to different parts of the world had come to take quite an interest in primitive mythologies. It was no different here. In fact it was a perfect opportunity during the long evenings here at the building site to pump his workers for tales of the local gods.'

'It was not long before he discovered that one of them was very local. The god was a "she", a witch-goddess, a kind of wild shaman woman of the hills. They told him that though with the coming of the Europeans the gods or spirit people were not as active, they were still present and that some of their people had sworn they had seen her: and they told him that she was a powerful woman, a huntress and magician.'

Klaus fell silent. All the time he was talking in that even tone of his, he had been turning the small dark leather packet (which I realized contained the letters he spoke of) over in his hands, but now, he held it motionless and stared down at it. I broke into his solitude, 'Why didn't he finish building the house?'

'He saw her.'

'The witch-goddess?'

'Yes, he wrote of it to my father — one moment, I'll read you what he, himself, said about it.' Klaus opened the leather packet, slid his hand in and carefully pulled out a small tattered bundle of yellowing envelopes. Opening one from the top he read from its contents in a slightly halting way as he translated the contents: 'I was coming back from the village late yesterday evening, quite late. It was dark but there was a full moon. I moored my small boat at the steps and was making my way back up to the building site. I came to the top, a high point along the trail that overlooks the creek, and was starting to make my way down when I sensed a movement in the largest of the pools below. I stopped and crouched low thinking I might have an easy shot at a deer in the moonlight for I carry my rifle with me at all times. But it wasn't a deer, of course, it was her, the shaman woman I told you about. She was bathing, her light flesh swaying and dipping like sculptured sandstone in the dapples of shadows and moonlight. Her long, willowy body was exquisitely beautiful. I lost sense of how long I watched, but I did watch to the end when she emerged to dress on the shore and then slip as silently and gracefuliy as a deer into the forest above her. She did not see me.'

Klaus stopped reading but he continued to talk as he carefully put the letter back in the packet, 'My grandfather was totally overwhelmed by the experience. Waking and sleeping he became obsessed with her. He lost all interest in the house, in his hunting; he dismissed all the Indians working for him. He wanted the whole valley to himself. The thought of his wife coming out became intolerable to the point when he finally wrote and forbade her to and then stopped writing to her. He continued communication to my father a little longer: letters filled with the obsession to see this woman again, and then they stopped.'

'Naturally his wife sent someone to talk to him, to convince him to come back to Germany, but he was impossible and would not talk to anyone. That was the last anyone saw of him, ever; and these letters I have would have been lost if I hadn't accidentally found them in an old chest of drawers that was being thrown out.'

'What happened to him, do you think?' I asked.

He paused briefly and replied: 'Do you think that passion . . . emotion, is a flaw?'

'If you mean that this obsession for the witch, if she existed, was one of passion, then perhaps it is. I rather think,' I said, 'that he was mad.'

'But if it were true. Do you think he had the right to destroy everything for this passion? The family went bankrupt without him. My grandmother was heartbroken.'

'I think he was mad. You can't blame a mad man for anything. They just are.'

'That's why I'm telling you all this,' he said suddenly.

'Why?'

'I want a witness to his madness.'

He placed the leather packet back in his bag and began to carefully repack it. 'It's time we got going.'

We started back down and by the time we had reached the intersection where the trail headed up over the ridge, the evening had reached that point of indecisive light when, for some reason, it is always very difficult to focus one's eyes. Everything becomes confused by a speckled grey and light phantoms move around the fringes of vision.

The trail forked off at the edge of the largest pool. I could not help feeling uneasy as I looked at it and thought of Klaus' witch-goddess. I wanted to stop for a moment, but after a very brief survey Klaus headed up the ridge. I thought he was anxious to get back to the boat before dark but when we reached the clearing at the top, which had given us our first view of the stream, he stopped.

'I'm going to stay here tonight. If you wish to remain with me, feel free to; I have enough warm clothes for both of us. If you don't want to, would you please return for me tomorrow morning with the boat? That is all the time I hope to need.'

His statement unsettled me. Though I was curious enough down by the pool to want to have a longer look, there was still enough little boy in me to be affected by 'ghost' stories. I was feeling quite happy to be on my way out of there and back to the warm lights and people at the Inn. I thought I knew why Klaus wanted to stay and my first reaction was to let him have the place to himself if he wanted it. But then the other part of that little boy came out, that part that said, back when I was sitting by the campfire years ago and hair was starting to prickle the back of my neck, 'Look behind you, look behind you into the darkness.' I stayed.

We settled down on a small patch of grass at the edge of the clearing. It was sheltered by low bush but still had a clear view down at the pool which was now fast losing its definition in the encroaching night. The pool was large only in comparison to others along the stream. At the outside it was perhaps thirty feet across. It fell off steeply at the edges though, and was at least six feet deep for most of its expanse. On our side it was bordered by a few feet of uneven gravel but on the far side there was a level ridge of sandstone perhap ten feet wide that went right up to the edge of the forest. A large arbutus tree leaned out over this ridge which was lightly dusted with leaves. It was a wonderful swimming hole.

Klaus gave me a sweater which I put on, though I hardly needed it, for the evening was warm and soft. He broke out some more sausage and bread, and a thermos of coffee. We ate and drank in silence and watched the night sink slow and deep into the forest around us. After we finished, I tried to begin a conversation but Klaus would have nothing of it. He hushed me silent. The night in the forest is strange company without the voice of another man. It is like lying alone and listening to the settling of a strange old house. Every creak and groan becomes more than it is. The normal physical functions of gravity and temperature change become animated with malevolent spirits. There in the trees the bushes creaked or swished unexpectedly and for reasons one could only speculate about. Slowly, however, the overwhelming presence of the night forest created a kind of peace in me and I relaxed and settled into it.

Klaus hardly moved but I could sense him in the dark and I could hear his steady breathing. The air was very still, though occasionally a light breeze moved through the trees like a wave.

I fell asleep and probably would have slept the rest of the night if Klaus had not had his dream. He must have woken both of us at the same time with his cries. When I started awake I was looking directly into his staring face, now well defined in the moonlight. His eyes were wide open but I had a feeling he was not looking at me but at some dream vision, as if he was having trouble escaping it.

I slowly dragged myself into a sitting position. My body was stiff and chilled through and through. 'Are you alright?' I said.

He mumbled something thick and incoherent. I watched him visibly compose himself.

'You were dreaming,' I said.

His face was very white in the moonlight. His throat was moving regularly as if there was great effort involved for him to answer me. 'I'm okay now,' he said, his voice a low rasp, 'just a dream, a dream.'

I got the canteen and handed it to him. 'What was it?' I said.

'I dreamt that I was shot through the back,' he said in a low controlled tone.

'By who?'

'I was being hunted.'

'Who was hunting you?' I said.

He huddled into himself for a moment and then slowly straightened out and looked around him. 'It's odd isn't it,' he said, 'I very seldom dream at all.'

He suddenly looked at me, 'How long were we sleeping?'

'Three or four hours, I don't know.'

'Please, be quiet, there can't be much time left.'

'For what?' I said.

He had crawled to the edge of the clearing and was looking down towards the stream. I noticed for the first time that he had his rifle out, cradled under his arm. 'Look at it, Mr. Clarke. Isn't it beautiful?'

The moon was almost straight above us now and the valley was luminous in its vibrant white light. All the fabric and contour of brush and trees were intricately defined by the sharp contrast of the light and the rich black shadows. Below, the creek was a constantly changing dance of light. I was mesmerized as I followed it with my eyes down to the pool which stood like a centre piece to the whole scene. The sandstone ledge stood out with a special whiteness while the laced shadow of the arbutus broke the water up into a web of light and dark that shifted in a light breeze. I could not take my eyes off it, and stared motionless — almost without thought. Then I saw her.

I was surprised and yet not surprised for her fine slender body appeared so much a part of the scene that her presence seemed inevitable; in fact, necessary to it. She walked gracefully across the ledge to the pool's edge where she dropped the light wrap she wore and then slipped into the pool like a sigh.

I heard Klaus shuffle beside me. He was breathing hard. I turned towards him. He was lying flat on his stomach and had his rifle to his shoulder.

'You're not going to . . .,' my voice cracked and halted.

'Be silent and don't move,' he whispered, 'and don't let her see you!'

I wanted to stop him somehow, push the gun aside or something, but I couldn't make myself. I was paralyzed by the strangeness of it all: the valley, the woman, Klaus. I turned back in a crouch and braced myself for the blast of the gun. I could see her sliding and twisting through the water: her body crisscrossed with the brocade shadow of the Arbutus tree. And then I sensed another presence by the pool — a deeper shadow among the shadows at the forest's edge. I heard Klaus catch his breath. He had seen it too.

A massive buck deer slowly, proudly, made its way down and out onto the ledge, its head crowned with a dazzle of antlers: curled and twisted and ancient. The witch-goddess was looking up at it: motionless. It was like an illustration from an old book of children's tales. Slowly, languidly, the woman started to make her way up onto the ledge toward the stag, her black hair in a long splayed wave down her back. She reached her hand out to it and the stag bowed its great head to meet her caress . . . suddenly it jerked violently back against itself and my whole sensibility was submerged in a raging howling sound as Klaus' shot carried and crashed wildly into the valley filling it with a violence, a roaring shock-wave reverberating without end. I felt a hand on my shoulder forcing me to the ground, 'Don't let her see you. Get down, get down. Don't let her see you!' Klaus hissed.

I could taste dirt and my face was suddenly hot with tears, 'You murdered him, you murdered him,' I kept repeating over and over again: muttering it into the ground, 'You murdered him.'

Klaus kept his arm hard down on me for what seemed like hours. The quiet of the forest returned but my mind continued to rage with the vision of the woman and the stag until that was all there was. Finally I felt a lightening of pressure on my back. I pushed his arm off me and painfully raised myself up. I said something confused to Klaus who was still on the ground, one hand clasping the gun, but he didn't respond. I bent to listen to his breathing. He was asleep.

The stag lay on the ledge by the pool, a motionless dark hulk. The woman was gone. The valley continued to shimmer in translucent light but I wanted no more of it and turned to stumble down the twisted half-light of the forest trail back to the boat where I collapsed into a dreamless sleep, cradled in its rocking.

I awoke the next morning with Klaus standing over me. I'm not sure whether he had made an effort to wake me or that somehow in my sleep I sensed his nearness. I remember that I had some difficulty understanding where I was or what had gone on before, and even when it started to come back to me everything seemed distant and unreal. I felt thick and drugged. Klaus motioned to shore, 'Will you help me with this?'

I pulled myself up and made my way on deck and squinted into the bright morning sun. Klaus had made his way onto the steps and was dragging something inch by inch down towards the water. It was the massive head of the stag. He stumbled and almost fell and then, looking up, shouted at me to help him. I didn't move, but only stared on in a dream. I had a sudden vision of Klaus, in the moonlight, crouched on the ledge butchering the animal, the sandstone stained black; Klaus agonizingly dragging his bloody, staring trophy up the ridge and down along the dark trail; Klaus crouched silently at the top of the steps, guarding the thing as he waited for morning.

And now here in front of me, Klaus grunting out the last feet down the jagged barren steps. I stared at him and the massive head with its thick, wide cluster of antlers.

He seemed to be expending great effort to move the thing. It was as if the head was heavier than it should have been, as if the steps had a kind of power that held their victim within the reality they also gave access to.

Quietly and methodically I cut the lines to shore and pushed the boat off. Klaus only became aware of it when I started the engine, but by then it was too late. He made a lunge out toward me and half fell into the water, ending up clinging waist deep to the final step: the head perched above him, antlers spread out like wings. I turned away and looked out over the calm open water. I didn't look back.

The Hot House

Claudette Charbonneau-Tissot
Tr. by Michael Bullock

EVERYTHING WAS GREEN in this room, the armchairs, the tables, the carpet and all these troublesome plants which, if the session didn't soon come to an end, were going to assail us with their climbing stems that would twine themselves round our ankles, our wrists and compel us to continue this difficult lesson until death ensued.

Perhaps he had brought me to this hot-house precisely because he believed that here it would be easier to act upon me as he acted, in this same place, upon the fragile seedlings of the exotic and delicate plants he cultivated.

I was beginning to suffocate in this overheated room. I asked him if I could open one of the windows that looked out on the garden, which was even greener and even more encumbered with leaves and flowers than the room.

He replied that none of them opened. And he immersed himself once more in this game that I was no longer able to follow, being too preoccupied with this moisture-laden atmosphere that made the sweat break out in beads on my forehead.

Although I knew that nothing was supposed to interrupt the game, I suddenly rose and asked him if it was possible to move into another room or put off the end of this game until later.

He nodded agreement.

Without even knowing which of the two proposals he had agreed to, I made my way to the door. But I couldn't open it.

Perhaps it was the moisture on my hand that made it slip on the door-knob. I felt as if I was going to faint or even die, drowned in this room in which the air was systematically changing into water.

I looked round at the gaming table. They hadn't moved, as if they had turned to stone as soon as I rose. K was still holding a mah-jong piece in his left hand, and in his right a cup of the tea that stood simmering on the tiny hot-plate which only increased the unbearable heat of this room.

I told him I couldn't open the door.

He asked me if I wanted some more tea.

I began to lose patience and told him I wanted to leave.

As if he hadn't heard, he told me it was still very hot.

This time I shouted that I wanted to leave.

He put down his cup, crossed his hands and, as if I wasn't there, he concentrated on the pieces in front of him. His forehead was dry and his breathing normal, like that of the other players. Perhaps they belonged to some amphibian species, so that they had no way of understanding the state of suffocation I was in.

I went up to K and begged him, in a low voice, to open this door on whose knob my hand slipped because it was wet.

He discarded the green dragon.

I turned round and was about to go back to the door when I saw, at the bottom of my cup, among the leaves, a whitish deposit which was not sugar and which must have contributed to the strangeness of the taste of this exotic tea, the particular variety of which K told me he chose himself each time.

I showed him the cup and asked him what that was at the bottom.

'Tea,' he replied with a smile. 'Didn't you drink tea just now? Perhaps you would like a little more to warm up what's left at the bottom of your cup?'

I didn't answer and put the cup down on the table.

A continuous buzzing started in my head as if it had suddenly been invaded by a swarm of bees. Little by little, these insects began to dance before my eyes until my vision was completely blurred. I dropped onto the rattan sofa and plunged into green water full of pondweed and lotuses.

WHEN I RETURNED to the surface, I was somewhere else, stretched out on a rush mat in a room with no other vegetation than that on the wallpaper, where tiny birds rested their thin claws on the interlaced branches of jasmine.

I rose with difficulty and immediately made for the door, which opened easily. I found myself on one of the landings of a tenement house which not only had nothing oriental about it but was not even situated in the Chinese quarter.

Once in the street, I walked as far as the nearest intersection, where I hoped that the names of the streets would enable me to draw the co-ordinates that would give me my exact position. But the two street names were unknown to me and therefore no help in finding my way in this district which, while it resembled the districts familiar to me in its buildings, its traffic, its posters and its pedestrians, seemed to me, through the mere fact that I didn't know where I was, almost as strange as if it had been a district of Shanghai.

I boarded the first bus that stopped at this intersection. The conductor told me I was going in the right direction to make the connection that would take me home.

I sat down on the first seat, near the door.

It was hot.

Little by little, my eyelids grew heavy and I couldn't fight sleep.

I don't know how long the journey took. I woke with a start when the conductor told me I had arrived.

I got up, still completely stupefield, and hurried out of the vehicle, which immediately closed its door and drove off.

The sun had gone a long way down.

I looked around me. There was no other bus line than the one I had just got off and I recognized nothing in this new place, not even the street names.

Perhaps the conductor hadn't understood my question. Or perhaps I hadn't even asked him my way home. My mind was still confused by all these insect larvae K had caused to hatch in me when he introduced the swarm of bees into it, and I didn't even try to clarify the situation.

I started to walk, at random, hoping that one day I would find a clue capable of transforming the alien universe in which I was walking with no other aim than to escape from this particular place, into a familiar universe in which every step would take me somewhere.

And this happened, when night had already fallen and I had been walking for a very long time. There it was, almost identical to everything I had been seeing for hours, since they were the same advertisements for cigarettes, soft drinks and gasoline, similar groceries offering the same canned goods, the same tobacco, but this time there was that little difference in the arrangement of each of these things, in this or that detail, which meant that this was no longer just any old place but this particular place, which I recognized and could situate in relation to others.

From that point on, I was able to find my way back to my apartment.

When I got there, I immediately stretched out and went back to sleep, drawn by something heavy inside me which not merely relieved me of all worry and all curiosity regarding what had happened to me, but also dragged me down into sleep like a stone tied round my neck. I did not resist this force.

WHEN I WOKE next day I had an ice-cold shower to rouse me from this torpor that I had been unable to shake off since the afternoon on which, as I had been doing for some time, I went to K for a mah-jong lesson.

After trying in vain to fill in on my own the gap of two days in my memory, I decided to go back to K to try and find the missing parts.

I picked up my handbag and was getting ready to go out when I suddenly saw, in its usual place, my mah-jong set, which had been on K's table at the moment I lost consciousness.

Someone else had brought it here, unless I had done so myself without realizing it, as I had perhaps also done with my car, which I found in its usual place.

I did sometimes confuse reality and dream and vice versa, imagining I had done something I had only dreamed and imagining I had dreamed something I had really done.

At times I even went so far as to create breaches in reality in order to insert in them a fragment of dream capable of breaking the monotony of everyday life.

It was a game.

But I had been doing this for such a long time that it had become almost automatic, so that now I sometimes allowed myself to be deceived by it.

Perhaps this had happened once again.

I pushed all these riddles to the back of my mind and headed for the town centre.

I parked the car quite a way from K's home, outside the Chinese quarter, and made the rest of the journey on foot so as to give myself time to prepare for this meeting, not knowing yet whether I ought to talk to K about my fainting fit, the memory blank that followed and my dangerous mania for confusing dream and reality, just for fun, or whether, on the contrary, I ought to act as if nothing had happened, as if I had simply come to continue the interrupted lesson, and wait for him to start talking about these things, or whether again I ought to assail him with questions the moment the door opened, asking him what he had put in the tea I had drunk, what had happened to me after that and how the mah-jong set and the car had got back to their places.

I reached K's house and chose the second solution, even if it meant reverting later to the first or the second.

I rang the bell.

K's servant opened the door. He wore the enigmatic smile that never left him, almost as if it was a theatrical mask glued to his skin, a mask, incidentally, of which there must have been several replicas, since even K sometimes used to wear it, without my ever being able to determine why he was wearing it on that particular occasion, because he was just as likely to adopt this smile when he said hello to me as when he reproached me with a bad move in the game or questioned me about my travels or my journalistic activities.

The servant asked me to wait in a tiny parlour I had never been in before, a kind of miniature museum in which were gathered bronze chimeras, tea bowls of fine porcelain, jade phoenixes, ink and wash drawings of mountain landscapes and pagodas. Some of the items seemed to be very old.

I didn't hear him coming in his embroidered silk slippers of very faded pink. He had that smile which narrowed his eyes more than usual and suddenly it seemed to me that all this too was part of a dream, unless K was quite simply a wax figure come to take his place in this collection of fossils.

As if nothing had happened, he took me into the green room where, although it was neither the day nor the time, the two other players were sitting (perhaps they were only robots whom K shut up in a cupboard and only took out when he needed someone to play with) and the tea was already on the hot-plate.

The two old men rose and greeted me together, bowing slowly, very low.

K invited me to sit down and served me a cup of that tea which, this time, I had decided not to drink, not wanting to be caught twice in the same trap and not wanting to miss anything of what was about to happen. I put the cup down on the table, close to the hot-plate, while he filled their cups and then his own, nodding his head slowly up and down and retaining that smile which now seemed to me slightly mocking, although to tell the truth I couldn't spot any detail that differentiated it significantly from his usual smile.

After putting down the teapot and taking a sip of tea, K lifted the lid of the mah-jong set that I had put on the table, opened the drawers one by one and began to take out the tiles, the underside of which was made of bamboo and the upper part of ivory and on which were painted, according to the function of each piece, a figure, a character or a number.

Each of his gestures seemed to form part of an unfailing ritual, so that it appeared to me now completely senseless to imagine that, three days ago, something could have interrupted the sequence of his gestures, impossible to believe that K would have allowed anything to disturb the established procedure of the scene which he reproduced faithfully every time I came for a session of instruction.

FOR A LONG TIME now I had ceased to be able to distinguish K from the achetypal image I had of the oriental master and I had often imagined that, when the lesson was over, K changed into bronze and remained like that until my return, unless that other old man whom I had once met as I was leaving the house, and who looked so much like K that you would think he was cast in the same mould, as did the other two old men by the way, unless this other old man came to take my place in the game and all four went on playing until I came back, without ever getting hungry or tired, content to play and drink this ambrosia tasting of tea that seemed never to run dry at the bottom of the tea-pot.

The sun came in through the windows and although it was neither cool nor dry I did not feel I was suffocating and there were no beads of sweat on my forehead.

We played for a long time and K made no allusion to the previous lesson and I did not dare refer to it, almost convinced, now, that I had dreamed it all and had mistaken my dream for reality.

When K replaced the bamboo and ivory tiles in the box, he told me he had to go away for a while and would not be able to see me. But a man would get in touch with me and would continue the mah-jong sessions with me, so that I shouldn't lose the skill I had acquired with so much hard work.

The servant was already there. K and his look-alikes rose and bowed deeply to me. The servant took the set from the table and put it in my hands.

And I found myself outside, at the door of the house, knowing almost nothing more than a few hours earlier, when I stood in front of this door in the same way I was standing now, with the mah-jong set under my arm, so that, for a moment, I had the impression that I hadn't yet entered K's house today, and I imagined I was still free to choose between the three solutions: whether to talk about my fainting, about nothing at all or about being kidnapped. To convince myself that this was only an illusion, a trick of my mind, I knocked at K's door again. A few moments later K's servant opened it and, before I had time to say a word, told me that K had had to go away for a while and that he wouldn't be able to see me.

But I knew that K hadn't had time to leave and certainly couldn't have gone out without my noticing, since I hadn't left his doorstep, unless he had gone out through the back door, which opened onto an alley filled with garbage, which would have been surprising, so that either he must be inside and didn't want to see me (perhaps he had already changed into bronze) or, but I hesitated to believe this, this was the first and not the second time I had knocked at his door that day.

I couldn't bring myself to turn around and go home, so I told K's servant that I thought I had left a mah-jong piece behind when I was there just now, the green dragon to be exact.

The mask came off his face for the first time, for the fraction of a second. He remained silent for a moment, then he said he would go and see if the piece was still lying on the table.

He went off and I immediately took a few steps in order to glance into the miniature museum, where most of the rare objects seemed to have been replaced by plastic replicas on whose bases, if I had not been afraid of the servant's return, I felt sure I should have found labels saying MADE IN JAPAN.

I barely had time to go back to the door when he reappeared. Automatically, I looked at his feet. I imagined it was embroidered silk slippers that made them as silent as K's, but instead of slippers I saw under the fabric covering his legs the thick crepe soles of shoes in a current style.

He told me he hadn't found the missing piece.

He took the mah-jong set from my hands, put it on the table, lifted the wooden lid and opened one of the drawers. There was the green dragon, between the red one and the white.

He said perhaps it was another piece that was missing.

He immediately opened all the drawers.

No piece was missing.

I stammered excuses.

He had recovered his mask. He returned the set to me and I went out, embarrassed.

A strange sensation came over me and my mind was filled with a chaotic mingling of the atmosphere of Malraux's books and images of the Blue Lotus opium dens.

To this was added the picture of K, when he was still in England, sitting at a mah-jong table where the stake consisted of this house whose threshold I had just left.

I tried to imagine this other scene, unable to remember whether it also formed part of what L, before introducing me to K, had told me about him, or whether it too was something I had made up. So I tried to imagine the scene, which must have taken place in England, or perhaps in China, in which the two Chinese who always made up the party during my practical mah-jong lessons, when they were completely ruined, had become the stake in a game of mah-jong which K had won.

And I had often wondered, as I entered that room in K's house in which I had taken my first mah-jong lessons, where the only furniture was four gaming-tables, chairs and an immense glass-fronted cupboard containing a mah-jong collection, whether all these sets had not been acquired in the same manner, that is to say when the opponent, ruined, had nothing else to wager but his mah-jong set and his soul.

Suddenly, I felt I might perhaps have gone too far in my imaginings. I had lost all notion of the boundary between reality and dream and I no longer knew in which of these universes I was now swimming.

So I decided to stop imagining scenes and set about verifying certain facts capable of clarifying my situation.

I drove towards the unfamiliar district in which I had woken up the previous evening completely disoriented.

But I was no longer too sure whether I hoped to find those unknown streets and that tenement house on the second floor of which there was a room whose only furniture was the rush mat on which I had woken up; I was no longer sure whether I hoped to find those elements which would prove that something had really happened, or whether, on the contrary, I hoped not to find any trace of this room and of that nightmare walk, which on the one hand would prove that I had not been the victim of a kidnapping but which, on the other, would prove that I was the victim of a mental disorder which was perhaps worse than everything that might really have happened to me during those two missing days.

Suddenly, as I turned a corner, it seemed to me that I had passed this spot, although there was no precise sign to justify this impression, although I could find no detail, not even the name of the street, because even though I remembered having looked at several of the street names as I walked along, I couldn't recall any of them, although I couldn't identify a single detail that would have enabled me to find my way in this maze, through which I was now certain that I had walked the previous evening.

I set off down this street, but I soon felt that I was lost again and I decided to return to the exact spot that had aroused vague memories in me.

From this starting-point, I decided to pursue my search on foot.

And I started walking, guided solely by this impression.

When I moved into another street, the vague impression that I had been here before left me; I turned around and tried walking in a different direction, until this impression returned.

After more than an hour of this trial and error I felt exhausted and went into a Greek restaurant.

I hadn't even had time to order anything when I saw, through the greasy window of the restaurant, the tenement house I had been looking for all this time.

I immediately got up and rushed into the street, towards this house in front of which I had stopped as though by instinct, as if it had been prearranged that I should reach the requisite degree of exhaustion after walking the distance that brought me here.

I went into the tenement house, climbed to the second floor and found the door behind which I knew there was a room with walls whose paper had a pattern calculated to give anyone who was coming round from the effects of a drug stretched out in the middle of a room and looking through half-closed eyes, the impression that he had turned into a statue in a Japanese garden, whereas in reality there was neither cactus, nor shell, nor plaster pagoda with upturned roof on this wallpaper invaded by dry branches that would certainly break if you leaned on them or catch fire if you dropped a spark from a cigarette on them.

I turned the doorknob, but without result. My hand was so damp that it slipped on the metal sphere. I tried again, in vain.

Suddenly there were noises and laughter on the other side of the door.

I could have gone and hid under the stairs and waited until one of those inside decided to come out.

But that might have taken a long time.

So I decided to knock without further hesitation.

The door opened almost at once to reveal a woman outlined against a wall covered with a metallic paper bearing a geometrical pattern, strips of which still lay around the floor among paint pots, brushes and rolls of adhesive paper.

For the second time, perhaps the third, the woman asked me what I wanted.

I replied that I thought I had been to this apartment the day before and had left behind a piece from a game.

She turned to the man who was with her and asked him if he had seen what I was looking for.

He asked me to describe the piece and I described the green dragon, although I knew perfectly well it was in its place in the wooden mah-jong box, which was in the car.

As I looked with them I told them I preferred this modern wallpaper to the oriental wallpaper that had covered the walls the day before.

I expected them to talk about this wallpaper or even to deny that the wallpaper underneath had an oriental pattern. Then I would have had no means of checking that they were wrong except to pull off a piece of the new wallpaper, which they must have taken a great deal of trouble putting on in order to make sure that each line of the pattern on one edge met the same line on the other edge.

But instead of talking about the wallpaper the woman asked me if I knew the people who had lived in this apartment before them.

This question took me by surprise and I answered no.

At this they stopped and looked at me in astonishment.

The man asked me what I was doing in this apartment the day before, which by the way has been empty for several days, if I didn't know the previous owners.

I said someone had made an appointment to meet me here to return the game, which belonged to me and from which I had discovered later that a piece was missing.

They had become suspicious and I preferred to apologize and leave.

I left this house, which did indeed exist; and even if I hadn't got to see it, I knew that in one of the rooms of this house there really was, under a metallic wallpaper whose paste was not yet dry, another wallpaper covered with exotic vegetation that would soon wither and whose birds would shortly die from lack of air, water and light.

I took the first taxi that came by and had it drive me to the place where I had left the car.

But the car wouldn't start. It was almost night already and I

hadn't eaten anything yet and was exhausted. I took an amphe-
tamine, as I did almost every morning when it looked like being
a bad day, when the coffee had a bad taste, the last scraping of
rouge caked on my cheek, the typewriter refused to print a letter. Then I walked to the nearest garage, where they towed in
the car, which wouldn't be ready till next day.

I took another taxi and went home.

The door to the apartment was ajar.

I pushed it slowly, switched on the light and looked around
cautiously before entering.

There was no one there, but someone had been there and had
rummaged through the apartment, though without taking anything.

I phoned L and asked him to come over.

As soon as he arrived I told him these fragments of story
which I was unable to link together.

I had the feeling now that during the two days I couldn't remember someone had attached an invisible chain to my ankle,
perhaps even it was a tendril of one of those climbing plants
that were invading the green room in which I had lost consciousness, so that I now felt tied tight to this extraordinary story
of which, in fact, I knew almost nothing.

As if it were a puzzle in which he had not merely to place but
also to find the scattered pieces, L questioned me about my
meetings with K, and the way I had spent my time during the
last few days, not neglecting any area of my life and hoping that
one of my replies would yield a clue, a trail. But we got very little out of them.

Then he made some phone calls, one of which disclosed that
K had recently lost several buildings at mah-jong, among them
his house in Chinatown.

This was one more piece of the puzzle, but we didn't know
what to do with it or where to place it.

We put the whole thing off until tomorrow.

L stayed with me that night.

SUDDENLY A BELL RANG and I wondered where it came from,
since there was no burglar alarm, no telephone, not even a door
in the vast field in which I was breathlessly running among
stalks of maize.

L shook me violently and dragged me out of this dream, from
which I emerged as out of breath as if I had really been running,
which supported the theory I had often defended in arguments

with L, according to which dreams were a form of metempsychosis, of passing over into a world just as real and physical as the one in which we were at present.

L said it would be better if I were the one to answer the telephone.

L put his ear close to mine. I lifted the receiver and gave my name to the man at the other end, whose own name I couldn't catch, his voice was so nasal and his accent so strong. I had to ask him to repeat what he had said several times before I understood that it was the man K had told me about, who was to continue my mah-jong lessons. I was about to make some excuse, when he told me the lessons would continue to be in K's house and that we could have our first meeting that same day.

I thought at first I hadn't heard right, but I was too embarrassed to ask him to repeat it a third time and L nodded his head to tell me to accept.

I answered that I would go.

I hung up.

Something wasn't clear and I was frightened of going back to that house.

L said that he would go with me and keep an eye on me, from a distance.

It was only when I was on the doorstep of K's former house and had rung the bell that I realized I didn't have my mah-jong set with me. I had left it in the car, in the garage. The man who had phoned me certainly had one of his own, or he would choose one from the glass-fronted cupboard, unless K had taken them all with him. In fact this detail didn't matter much, because I had come here not so much to play as to see the man who had made the appointment and try to cast some light on the mystery of the last few days.

A Chinese in western dress opened the door a crack. He wasn't smiling and I was suddenly sure I had misunderstood the telephone message, so that it wasn't the man who had called me a few hours earlier who was in the house, but the one who had beaten K at mah-jong and with whom I had nothing to do.

However, before I could turn round and start running, as in my early morning dream, he asked me my name and as soon as I had given it he put on the same mask as K's servant, opened the door wide and said I was expected.

It seemed to me now that if I crossed this threshold and let the Chinese close the heavy red door behind me, I should never

98

be able to turn back again and would enter not the time machine, but the space machine, so that I would soon be catapulted into a strange world where I should be the only one with white skin and eyes that were not slanting and where everyone would spend his time playing this game of which I should soon become the principal stake.

I turned my head slightly and looked to see if L was at his post behind the window of the restaurant, where I saw Chinese lanterns made of crystal paper covered with hieroglyphs and edged with a long red fringe that swayed in the puff of air from the fans. L wasn't there.

I turned towards the Chinese, who was waiting for me to go in, but without bowing like K's servant, who used to double up as I passed till his torso was almost at right angles to his legs. It was too late to turn back and I went in. The Chinese led me to the far end of the house. At each step his stiff shoes creaked. He showed me into the green room and asked me to wait a few seconds.

The arrangement of the room was unchanged and the gaming table, the green rattan sofa, the hot-plate and the tea bowls were still there; but there was something different in the air, which was no longer saturated with moisture and in which there floated a vague odour of decomposition. I soon noticed that the troublesome entangled plants were beginning to wither, although I hadn't noticed anything of the sort the previous day or the day before that.

I heard a creaking sound and I knew that the Chinese had come back. He was accompanied by another Chinese, quite young and dressed like him in western clothes though rather more elegantly.

He greeted me with a nod and introduced himself. He said a few words about K, who had had to go away for a while on business and who had entrusted him with the task of continuing my lessons in Chinese dominoes.

We were about to sit down, when he pointed out to me that I hadn't brought my mah-jong set.

I was on the point of replying that I had left it in my car, but then I would have had to explain that my car had broken down, that it was at the garage, which might have taken a long time and would certainly not have been of the slightest interest to this man. So I simply answered that I had left it at home.

He signed with his hand to the other Chinese and the latter went out.

Then he crossed his hands on the little table and remained silent.

His eyes were resting on me and soon I didn't know how to look.

Without thinking, I asked him if he had been here long.

I immediately realized how clumsy and even dangerous my question had been, because now that he had told me that K would be away from this house for some time, whereas I knew very well that he had lost it gambling (but perhaps L's information was wrong, or perhaps K had meanwhile won the house back), I suspected this man of being an impostor, although I couldn't think why he should have taken the trouble to lure me here or what he hoped to gain by it.

Before S had replied to my question, the servant came in with a black mah-jong box, which he must have polished before bringing it, because it was so shiny that otherwise it would have shown fingerprints.

After putting the box down on the table, he sat down on my right. Then the fourth player arrived and without being introduced or any exchange of words sat down in his turn.

S began to take the pieces from their tiny drawers.

Suddenly, when I was no longer expecting an answer, S said that he had been here for some years and that he was K's son.

Then I tried to imagine K copulating in his encumbering garments and his embroidered silk slippers that were like a second skin to him. I couldn't. Perhaps he had had recourse to artificial insemination.

We started to play.

From time to time, S asked me a question about the game in progress or about the way K had taught me to play. Then he asked me whether K sometimes, when the game was over, invited me to have a meal with him or took me into the garden.

He must have noticed my astonishment at these questions, because he told me his father hadn't said much to him about what he was supposed to do apart from getting me to play mah-jong.

When I told him that my meetings with K had always been limited to playing mah-jong and that as soon as the game was over I had always left, he seemed surprised. Then, with a knowing smile, he said that of course it would have been surprising if a woman like me had taken any other interest in the company of a man as old as his father apart from an educational one.

We had continued to play, but I saw that they were beginning to get impatient. Without moving their heads, they sometimes cast strange glances at each other. This, together with the ambiguous nature of the preceding remarks, gradually made me feel uneasy. Beads of sweat began to form on my forehead (although, this time, there was no tea on the switched-off hotplate) and before I was overcome by a feeling of suffocation, I decided, although it was sacrilege to interrupt the game and in spite of their mute disapproval, to go and wash in cold water.

I rose and left the room, followed by their heavy looks.

As I passed the room which K had dedicated to mah-jong I couldn't help lightly pushing the door, which was ajar. The mah-jong boxes were no longer in the huge glass-fronted cupboard but scattered all over the floor and on the gaming-tables, where the bamboo part had been detached from the ivory part of each piece with the aid of hammers and chisels, which were still lying there.

I heard the creak of shoes, far away, and I hurried to the bathroom, where I locked myself in.

I remained for a few seconds leaning against the door, holding my breath.

The creak of shoes drew near, stopped, then moved away.

Then I splashed my face.

The towel was on the floor.

I dried my hands and went out.

As I passed the mah-jong room I noticed that the door had been shut.

When I entered the hot-house room the three men were by the window, talking in low voices in their language. I no longer felt like going on with the game and hoped they would say as much. But they came back to the table and we went on playing.

At a certain moment I wanted to take a tissue from my handbag and I noticed that it had been closed with the press button, which I never used.

When the game was finished, S offered to see me home.

I was on the point of saying that L was waiting for me (unless he had got tired of waiting or had imagined that I had been swallowed up forever once I had crossed the threshold of this house), but I changed my mind and told him I had my car and was going to do some shopping before going home. When I was on the point of leaving, he told me (but it was more of an order than an invitation) to come back next day, at the same time, and that I had played very badly today and still had a lot to learn.

He didn't wait for my answer and shut the door.

I immediately looked for L behind the window of the Chinese restaurant where he had said he would wait for me.

He wasn't there.

So I walked in the direction of the car in which, feeling tired, he had perhaps sought refuge from the smell of the food that was being cooked around here.

The door wasn't locked. I sat down on the seat and waited for him, barely a few seconds. He had stopped under an arcade to look, from a distance, at a group of slit-eyed men playing mahjong in a courtyard.

We left that district and went for dinner in a quiet spot where we talked about my visit to K and the events of the last few days.

When we came out, a few hours later, the car was no longer where we had left it. We looked for it and, as we couldn't find it, L called up the police, who found it three-quarters of an hour later in a back street a few blocks away. The trunk and the glove compartment had been turned upside down and the seats ripped open.

The police made out a report asserting theft and vandalism, ignoring the points that did not agree with such a conclusion.

I would have liked to tell them that something else was involved, that we were mixed up in some strange business, that my apartment had been ransacked, but L lowered his eyes and gave me an imperceptible sign not to do so.

When it was all finished, we went to L's place.

It was only after I had been over the facts several times that I remembered telling S, who wanted to take me home, that I had my car. So it probably wasn't L's car they had wanted to search but mine.

I wanted to go to the garage where I had left it and where they must certainly have finished the repairs, which in any case was of no importance, since what I wanted at the moment was not to start the car up but to open up with a knife its seats covered in a common brocade, to search through the trunk and the glove compartment to see if they didn't contain something unusual.

L said that the people who were looking for this thing, to which we couldn't yet give a name, were probably waiting for this action on my part which would lead them to the object they were after, assuming that this object really was in my car. He was probably right.

He suggested that I should go back to my apartment, while he went to the garage and searched the car.

I PUT THE KEY in the lock and opened the door. The apartment had been ransacked once more. I immediately telephoned L, but he had already left. I was going to hang up when I heard the creaking of footsteps behind me.

The man with the noisy shoes was there and so was S, who took the receiver, listened and then, hearing nothing but the dialling tone, hung up.

He asked me where I had put what K had entrusted to me.

I said K hadn't entrusted anything to me.

He remained silent for a moment then, changing his mask and the subject, he said they happened to be passing and had come to play a game of mah-jong.

Then he asked me where my set was.

Immediately, in a flash, I saw the mah-jong set on the front seat of the car. I had forgotten all about it when I made a mental inventory of what was in the car.

S repeated his question, this time firmly.

I stammered that it must be here, in the kitchen or perhaps in the bedroom.

Without having to check my statement, since they had already searched the apartment, he told me that before I arrived they had wanted to play but hadn't found the set.

Without thinking, I said that anyway the game was usually played by four.

He started laughing, but at the same time his hand came down like a sabre on my left arm.

I found myself on the floor, my head buzzing. The numbness of the shock wore off almost at once and was replaced by pain.

Assuming a falsely contrite air, S apologized and bent down to help me up, but instead of taking me by my undamaged arm he grasped my bruised arm, I cried out, but he didn't let go until I was standing up.

He asked me again where the mah-jong set was.

This time I saw no reason to persist in defending this set which, in reality, didn't have as much value for me as it seemed to have for them.

I told them where it was.

They left immediately and at this moment, if it hadn't been

for the pain in my arm, I could have believed the whole thing had been merely a figment of my imagination.

The telephone rang and when I heard L's voice I suddenly realized that I had sent S and the other Chinese to the garage while L might still have been there.

L said he hadn't found anything unusual in the car but that he had brought back everything he could, including the mah-jong set.

I realized that as soon as they saw that the car had already been searched and that the mah-jong set was no longer there they were bound to come back. I told L, without giving him any explanations, to wrap up the mah-jong set and go to our usual meeting place, where I would join him as soon as I could.

I rang off at once, took my handbag and quickly opened the door behind which, unknown to me, the Chinese with the squeaky shoes was acting the watch-dog.

Without his having any need to take out a firearm, a knife or a sabre, the mere persuasion of the look that filtered out from beneath his folded lids made me back away into the apartment without daring to utter a cry or even a word of protestation.

He told me to sit down and I knew without any explanations from him that we were waiting for S, who was not long in returning, his eyes even narrower than usual in his anger.

The watch-dog spoke a few monosyllables to S, whose face seemed immediately to relax.

S turned to the third player and spoke a few words to him in his singsong voice. The third player immediately left the apartment.

S sat down in the green velvet easy chair and we stayed like that, waiting, though I didn't know what for. S now had his disquieting smile.

Suddenly, after more than ten minutes of silence and immobility, the phone rang.

The sweat began to run down my forehead as S rose and went to the telephone.

He lifted the receiver and after a few seconds of silence he uttered two or three sounds in his language and slammed it down again.

Again anger rendered his eyes almost invisible under his lowered lids. He came up to me and asked me where L was.

His question took me by surprise and I remained openmouthed.

Then he said the Chinese watch-dog was at L's apartment and L wasn't there.

I concluded that the watch-dog hadn't heard the meeting-place.

For the second time, S asked me where L was.

I couldn't take my eyes off his hand and I was afraid it would leap out and smash down on me again.

But I answered that I didn't know where L was.

S began to sway his head from left to right and from right to left, clicking his tongue in his mouth.

I closed my eyes and told myself it was time to wake up, to return to reality, to come out from this dream in which I was no longer taking any pleasure.

Suddenly there was an explosion inside me; I staggered and fell to the floor.

I opened my eyes and saw S's hand returning to his thigh.

I had made a mistake. The thing was not to return to reality but to get away from it before it was too late.

In spite of the violent pain in my arms, I closed my eyes and tried to go backwards in time, to flee this place, these beings, to get out of my body, to leave nothing there but an empty carcass, an abandoned hulk.

But S's hand was sufficiently long and hard to seek me out in this tunnel into which I was slipping with difficulty.

The hand leapt into action and reached me on the floor.

This time, the target was my face and I felt pieces of broken teeth inside my mouth.

Everything was going too fast now and I couldn't even manage to close my eyes, I was so afraid that S's hand would leap out again.

The telephone began to ring.

S said it must be L.

I wanted to get up and rush to that telephone, even though I wouldn't have known whether I ought to shout to L to come to my aid or, on the contrary, to run away and escape from these diabolical beings.

But I was incapable of getting up and S, who had gone over to the phone, was pressing the receiver as though better to feel the vibrations of the bell.

After a certain time, S lifted the receiver but without putting it to his ear.

From where I lay, I could hear L's voice over the phone.

Suddenly, realizing that they had forgotten to gag me, I began to shout L's name.

After a few seconds, S rang off.

I knew he was going to come over and start hitting me again, but his face was relaxed and he told me I had done exactly what he expected of me and that now L was bound to come.

Aided by the watch-dog, S stretched me out on the velvet chesterfield at the far end of the room facing the door.

S switched off a few lights while the watch-dog went to the kitchen and made tea.

When he came back, S took the cup in his hands and brought it to my mouth, in which I scarcely felt the scalding of this liquid as it flowed down my throat mingled with blood.

I would have liked to push the cup away, but I couldn't raise my arms or move my head from the cushion where S had placed it.

Little by little I felt the sweat return to my skin and I felt as though the liquid was running into my lungs instead of into my oesophagus. I began to cough painfully as if I were drowning in glaucous water full of pondweed and lotuses, into which I was gradually sinking but through which I nevertheless continued to see the watch-dog and S, who moved away from me, in slow-motion, then disappeared.

I felt no more pain now and I had the impression that I had really become an abandoned hulk. Perhaps I had succeeded in re-entering my dream, perhaps now I was safe.

I remained like this, fixed in this sweet eternity where there was nothing to do but stay stretched out, in pieces, on this green velvet chesterfield bathed in the soft light from the tortoise-shell lamp.

Dull thuds at the door slipped into this eternity without breaking its continuity. Then I saw the door slowly open to reveal L, who was carrying under his arm a packet wrapped in brown paper.

When he saw me he stopped moving and I thought that he too was going to be fixed in this position forever.

But he soon started running slowly towards me, as in an underwater ballet; then he bent over me as S appeared behind him, raised his hand and struck L on the nape of the neck, so that he slowly collapsed on top of me and then slid down onto the floor.

S and the watch-dog took the brown parcel and ripped the

paper from the mah-jong set that I had bought some time ago at an auction, not knowing that it contained a magnetic charm capable of attracting these yellow men, who switched on all the lights before taking out each of the pieces.

They spread out a large sheet of copying paper on which they put the pieces one by one before splitting them open like oysters, separating the bamboo part from the ivory part. From each piece came a white, crystalline powder which they at once slipped carefully into an envelope of the same paper.

Only the green dragon contained no powder. S took from it a tiny scroll of thin paper on which were written characters as incomprehensible as the monosyllables they exchanged.

When they had finished collecting the powder from the pieces, they sealed the envelope containing the powder and the other envelope in which they had put the tiles as they split them open. S put the tiny scroll in a small metal cylinder, which he slipped into the inside pocket of his jacket. Then they rose and left.

L and I were left alone, at the bottom of that warm, transparent water from which L emerged first but in which I remained for a long time after him, as in a dream, away from pain.

I was taken to hospital, where they made me pass quickly from the green, fluid, luminous water to a black, deep water into which I sank heavily.

I WAS RISING to the surface but still only half-way up when I had the feeling I was being mummified and wrapped in bandages. Soon I felt that I was a prisoner in a sarcophagus which I should never get out of.

When I came completely to the surface, my two arms were covered in plaster and a metal rod protruded from one of them.

A taut strip of webbing held my chin down so that I had to keep my mouth open.

The room was empty and I couldn't reach the bell that had been pinned to my bedcovers, but a little too high up.

I tried to call, but the strip of webbing holding down my jaw prevented me from forming any words. I uttered a few whimpering sounds, but without result.

There was nothing I could do but wait for someone to come.

But when the door finally opened, I regretted having hoped for this moment.

It was a slant-eyed man, in western dress, whose face seemed familiar even though I didn't recognize him. It was only as I saw him coming slowly towards me in his crepe-soled shoes that I recognized K's servant.

When he reached the bed, he bowed double in greeting, then straightened up.

Then he placed K's personal mah-jong set on the bed, or an exact replica, a very beautiful set of purplish-blue wood like rosewood, on which were painted tiny flowers in whose corollas minuscule birds seemed to be sleeping, unless they were dead, like those greedy bumble-bees that gorge themselves on pollen till they can't fly and then die on the ground.

The servant said that K was sending me this present because of the trouble he had caused me.

He said goodbye and left, without another word.

I looked with terror at this rosewood box full of dead birds, as if it were a deadly poison. I started to scream and tried to huddle up as close as possible to the head of the bed.

A nurse came in and, seeing me in this agitated state, at once called for help.

She took the box inside which, in each little drawer, there were no doubt hollow bamboo and ivory tiles inside which there were perhaps other little dead birds; she took the box and put it down on the bedside table.

She didn't seem to be contaminated by the contact as I had been by contact with the other set I had bought at the auction. But perhaps that was a long-term process, as it had actually been with me.

Suddenly the idea of breaking the spell by giving the mah-jong set to this stranger occurred to me and I tried to make her understand that she could take the box, that I was giving it to her, that I was making her a present of it.

But she couldn't make head or tail of my inarticulate groans and to put an end to my agitation she took a syringe from the little tray she had been brought. I tried to push it away because I didn't want to plunge again into glaucous water full of pondweed and dead fish.

But it was a wasted effort. The air began to grow heavy and the room was soon changed into a hot-house and then into an aquarium.

When I was completely submerged, they went out and left me alone again.

But while I was under water, S's men came in and carried me far away from the universe that was familiar to me.

AND I SOMETIMES WONDER if they haven't shut me up alive in one of the bamboo and ivory pieces of a gigantic mah-jong, with which some yellow gods are playing as they slowly sip a tea-flavoured ambrosia.

And when I hear someone crying out at night, I wonder if it isn't L who has been shut up in the next piece.

The Veteran

Derk Wynand

DEFYING THE VILLAGERS' BELIEFS about his physical capacities,
defying them deliberately and in vain — he knows they cannot
perceive his intentions — the veteran has climbed the tall fir
tree outside the cook's house, its bottommost branches too high
or dry-rotted to allow for a proper handhold, its trunk too large
to be scaled readily, even by a man not crippled by war injuries.
Without the aid of rope or ladder, he has managed to climb the
tree and he sits now in its branches, his thoughts not on defi-
ance.

Earlier in the day, he has watched the cook's wife in the market square. He has followed her from stall to stall. Unlike other
women — the more voluptuous barmaid, for instance, who has,
over the months, learned to ignore him, despite her ordinary
kindness, or the blacksmith's wife, who no longer stops to listen to his incomprehensible gurgling, no longer pretends to understand the sense that she once felt underlay it — the cook's
wife took the time to ask how he was progressing, as if she gen-
uinely cared, and so, he followed her home. Maybe she reminded and reminds him of a woman he knew in his youth,
reason enough for a man to chase after a woman. Or it is that he
vaguely remembers his former teacher's wife — how inaccessible she had always seemed — and that his old curiosity has sur-
vived the recent experiences that have erased many of his re-
membrances. Now it is evening. He has followed her, the
distance between them constantly increasing: his awkward gait,
his stumbling, and his sprawling into the dust after every third
or fourth step prevented him from keeping up with her. Perhaps he was afraid to intimidate her with his unsightly presence. Perhaps he lost sight of her entirely and merely followed a
distant memory.

It is evening. He sits in the fir tree's branches and does not
wonder how he has come to be here. His ragged green uniform,
soaked with the sweat of his recent exertion, does not protect
him from the increasing chill, which he ignores.

As he sits on a branch approximately level with the cook and
his wife's bedroom, his breathing gradually finds its normal

rhythm. He has managed to climb the tree, as though he had suddenly regained control over his constantly agitated limbs. His legs appear to have recalled their original function. His hands have remembered that they were created for other purposes than to swat the invisible projectiles that buzz always past his ears. His head, too, now filled only with visions of this woman in whom he places, unreasonably, so many of his hopes, has stopped twitching and jerking to avoid the less insistent projectiles. Why should he not place all his hopes on this woman, he thinks, as if someone had asked him, since they have not come to fruition elsewhere?

If any of the villagers saw him now, perched high in the branches, they would conclude that the veteran, a cripple who could barely manage a few consecutive steps without tripping over his own feet, had magically learned how to fly. But, tricked so often by the roving bands of gypsies, they would remember that they had lost faith in magic. Their eyes, they would say, are playing tricks on them again. No, even should they pass beneath the fir tree, should they happen to look up in passing, they would not see him, nor ask what he is doing there.

In recent months, the villagers have developed a certain blindness to the veteran, even when he spends his time in more likely places. Their ears have learned not to heed the gurgling babble that serves him as speech, poorly serves him, so often has he pestered anyone who pretended to understand with stories about his boyhood and his army days. At the village inn, he has talked all too frequently about his past, and the wine has not made his words any clearer.

How he excelled at jumping.

How his talents were immediately put to good use by his officers.

How he was a courier. And a scout.

How he leaped unharmed through the minefields.

How he climbed impossibly steep roofs or water towers to report on the enemy's position and movements.

And the other places to which his skills led him.

Dark rooms.

Black-haired women.

No gypsy could compare.

The friendly wives of the enemy.

Daughters.

Leaping. No, not minefields.

And his voice always dropped then, as he told of the barn

from the top of which he had been shouting down the information about the enemy's movements. Or the women's.

How it was already burning.

How no one could have foreseen that it would cave in so quickly.

How he was sent into the flames.

How he managed to escape, and for what?

And look at him now. Look at him.

The villagers looked at him. Sadly at first, they shook their heads to hear the unintelligible gurgling that issued at last from the cripple's mouth. But he has become painfully familiar. He has tried so often to make himself understood that no one, not even the barmaid, tries any longer to make sense of his slavering, which seldom approximates ordinary speech. Not even his ragged uniform wins him an audience now.

He leans back against the trunk of the fir tree, eases his weight onto a branch level with the cook's bedroom window. For the first time in months, his body feels comfortable, as if it were made to perch in trees. Growing increasingly chilled, he ignores the cold, for he is filled with anticipation. A vague memory stirs in him. He senses that he has sat on this branch before. At any moment, he knows, the light in the bedroom will be put on, giving substance to his visions. Eagerly, he anticipates what he will see in the soft lamplight only a few yards in front of him, since neither the cook nor his wife has drawn the curtain shut. Presumably, she will tell her husband that she likes to see the moon rise. It puts her in the mood. The veteran, however, can only guess her words and her motives; he prefers his own interpretations, which allow him a fragile hold on the world around him. He likes to think that their carelessness is a sign that they do not intend to exclude him from their lives.

As he watches them begin to shape each other in the wide bed, however, he realizes that he plays no genuine part in their intimacies. For all the effect he has on them, or they on him, he could be an angel, a mere catalyst in human affairs, his own nature not altered in the process. A rush of blood to the ears, yes, he feels that, even as an angel must when he witnesses the lesser activities. But he is no angel, despite the patience with which he watches, despite the occasional miracles his mind performs to entertain itself. He listens to the pulse in his ears slowly drown out the buzzing projectiles. He watches the cook render his wife into novel shapes. He gurgles and claps his hands for joy, then quickly takes hold of an overhead branch to keep from falling. It is not yet the occasion for falling. Time and again, he applauds one or the other of the two pliable creatures stirring on the bed. He wants to urge them on to still greater achievements, though he knows they can neither see him nor hear him.

The veteran can sit, invisible, even in the bright moonlight, outside a cook's bedroom window. Despite the brief moments of joy it brings him, however, he does not savour his invisibility as many a man has dreamed he would, if given the chance, for he realizes only too well that it is a dream from which there can be little hope of waking. Yet he has not always been invisible, and therefore he does hope. As he shifts restlessly on his branch, he does so as if this night offered him a final opportunity to prove himself a man of flesh and blood, someone who would have to be dealt with sooner or later, in one way or another.

Never taking his eyes off the cook and his wife — in the soft light, he sees them shape each other into owl and mouse, into snuffling dogs, into gently hovering creatures — he reflects on his recent life in the village. In his reflections, he knows, he runs counter to the villagers' beliefs about his capacities, for they have long come to equate his physical shortcomings with a mental infirmity. He acknowledges it as a necessary equation.

He looks back almost nostalgically to his arrival, his return to the village. His thoughts linger with special affection on the dogs that greeted him in the early morning. Again, he hears them growl, then go into a frenzy of barking as he lurches toward them. He falls heavily in the centre of the circle they have formed around him. One dog, its teeth bared, leaps forward, but it stops immediately when it notices that the others have not followed. Briefly, the veteran feels a sense of his own power: his stern gaze can hold back the fiercest of dogs. Then he knows better. All the dogs have begun to whine, averting their eyes from him, looking for their masters, who are not there to urge them forward. Now, he almost wishes that someone had been there to give the command that, though it would have finished him, would have proved him a man like any other. If only he had had the voice for it, he thinks now, he would have called the dogs upon himself.

In time, the dogs grew used to him, as their masters did. For some weeks, he placed all his hopes on the children. But they were frightened by the sight of his burned face. Blank, white scar tissue. Now, as he lurches again down the street, the children do not ape his clumsy walk, as he wants them to do. And even if they do lurch along behind him, swatting the air as he does, he cannot catch them at it. Never can he turn quickly enough to catch them, nor is he sure that he wants to: he prefers the certainty of his vision of them to the likelihood that they have already tired of the easy sport. Yet he knows they no longer fall silent when he approaches. For them, he has become a sight more familiar than the solitary trees along the village street.

The veteran emits a loud, pained sigh. He is startled by its volume, though the cook does not pause in his strenuous efforts to maintain the new shape of his wife's breast. She too makes no sign that she has heard anything unusual. Silent once more, the veteran turns his thoughts from the children and the dogs to their parents and masters, who have ignored him almost from the outset, with the exception, perhaps, of the barmaid and the blacksmith's wife, and a few drunkards at the inn, who know what it means to be ignored. When he feels charitable toward them, he attributes their neglect of him to their rational or sensitive natures.

On the other side of the window pane, the owl spots the mouse in the shadows. The dog, dancing on its hind legs, settles finally onto the bitch, that no longer snaps and snarls at him. The hovering creature slowly eases itself onto the other. The veteran rubs his eyes. His hand grows numb; he supports himself with the other hand. He shifts his weight from one buttock to the other. Through the window that separates him from the cook and his wife, he sees the owl flutter up and come to rest, sated. The dog tires of its dance. The hovering creature turns on its side and rests on its folded wing. The veteran rubs his eyes. He watches the cook's breathing become regular, as his wife sits up in bed. She looks down at her breasts, which are gradually returning to their former shape. He sees her get out of bed to examine herself in the mirror. It is clear to him that she cannot accustom herself to the changes her husband always manages to effect in her, despite the number of times he must have done so already. He watches her approach the window and stand there, naked, and his body inclines toward her. It is the moment he has waited for.

He shakes the branches above his head; he imitates the hooting of an owl. He sees the cook's wife tilt her head slightly, as if she has noticed a movement in the branches, or some shadow that does not belong among the familiar shadows. He knows it is his own interpretation, as his invisibility is. His body begins to reassert itself. His hands swat the empty air. He senses that he must fall, that his body wills it, and his mind gives in, as it always does. His eyes fix the naked woman in the window, even as he wobbles precariously on the branch. His hand slowly loosens its grip, and he tells himself that he is releasing it. He begins to fall, but not before he has seen the cook's wife draw the curtain shut. Now he wants to fall. He is losing his grip. He takes her action as a sign. He knows he is deluding himself, knows that she has merely grown uneasy in the moon's harsh light, but he clings to his stubborn interpretation even as he crashes into the lower branches, which hardly break his fall. Only his interpretation matters, he thinks. Accordingly, the cook's wife has recognized him. He has been recognized. In the seconds left him, he hopes that she will find him at the base of the tree in the morning, she or anyone else.

Four Prose Poems

Robert Priest

THE KISS I JUST MISSED

The kiss I just missed giving you wound up later on another mouth, but by then it had become a little cold and cruel. It wanted to be just burned off in sunbursts and cleansed of its longing. It imparted only melancholy. Where it goes now I don't know. Probably to be used and used on other mouths. Each time worn down a little more like a coin to its true longing. Perhaps it will reach you then from some impartial lover — from some dispassionate goodbye — like a stem cut from its rose.

That kiss that didn't make it to your mouth made it instead to Toronto, for I could not be rid of it in Palo Alto. It stained my lips even in Mendocino. In a Triumph Spitfire I could not by singing out the window leave a long burning stream of it hissing in the blue air. It has become an irreconcilable wound now. A grand comparer. It lands on lips in a regular autumn but it will never be severed from its mouth. I wash it in water — it is there. I wash it in wine — still it is there. Drunken then, singing your name, mouthing it hot and burning into my mind it has shown me its red edges, its arms and legs that didn't go round. It has talked to me sadly of clothes, of beds it didn't lie down in. What a weeper! It has dragged me under rain. Indelible. Indelible. Wants to go finally to the graveyard of old kisses, each one with its denied rose strolling ghostly over. Each one with its sunset nova quenched in amber on its headstone. O each of its stopped explosions driven down to juice in some white withering berry there.

I knew a man who wore his little mother on a chain round his neck. You might say she had pierced ears. Often she would turn around in rage and bite him, but due to the fact that he had tied her little hands behind her back, her teeth couldn't harm him. As can be expected, this strange behaviour of his did not prevent him from adopting all the newest philosophies of the day. Indeed, this fellow even claimed to be what is called a Women's Libber. So eloquent could he become on this subject that he was regarded by some as something of a saint. Yet, even as he spoke, even as he decried aloud the centuries of cruelty and injustice to women, he would raise his hand to his chest as though in religious gesture and begin to pinch his little mother. He did this so that her tiny screaming might add fuel to his rhetoric. On those nights when he did not bring liberated women home to fuck, he would untie her long enough for her to call him an ungrateful bastard. 'I'm sorry, mother,' he would say serenely, 'but whatever I am, you have made me. Now go and do your business.' After she had done her business, he would clothespeg her little legs together so that he could get to sleep.

The pear likes to stuff it down. Left alone long enough, it will eat even its own roots. And *its* roots of all roots are the most grasping, the most malicious in their search underground for things to eat. The pear is aware only of the tip of its pointy head — that fat bulge beneath is an abscess into the subconscious to it. It likes to rock on it when it spouts its pointy-head opinions. Pears are the most socially distraught of all fruit. Their buttock blindness leads them always into surrogate maternity, self-pity, secret scoffing and the running of poetry readings. The pear is opinionated. It thinks everything lithe or white or dancing is disgusting. It drinks from tea cups. It fingers itself secretly and hones down all its 'poetries' to no more than one page. The pear has discharge at night when it dreams of being lecherous or fucked. But the pear has no cunt. It never did. It just eats and absorbs and lies about its weight, wishing that some little seductive bit of itself could stick out of something and titillate somebody. Pears usually live in countries. They are usually extremely nationalistic. You will find them in universities or lavatories. For all their scoffings and scorns the pears are basically dull and sheepish and will believe anything anyone with a degree tells them. The pear would be forgivable but it is responsible in its own way for the starvation of the prunes on a worldwide scale. If you mention this it will talk of self-determination, of right to life, birth control and free will. Then it will eat another turtle. It will get fatter without a blush right before your eyes. Sometimes you will find a half-digested child inside a pear. Pears should be hung up on hooks. They should be made to bleed through the tip of their pointy heads. Whenever you bite into a pear you should do so slowly, savagely, saving that shrill pointy head to the very end.

1 The Vanishing Brassiere

The vanishing brassiere hung down in the conscience of the 'monogamist' with no tits to fill it. If he thought of Fuck, it was the wind whistling over a razor's edge, FFFFFFFFFF, and then a tympani of nuts falling onto tin cans, K-K-K-K-K-K! Like the cratered eyes of some dog he'd maimed, that brassiere haunted him. When would it reappear and relieve him of the ballast of his guilt? Always, no matter what he was doing, he was searching for it and everything that came between him and finding it easily was a razor. The clock was a razor. Every evening was a razor. His wife was a razor — especially his wife, whom he had used over and over again without, he thought, in the least dulling her wit. It was still pebble sharp. But how she slashed him from the mainstream. How she cut him at the wrist of the world. How, where tits should be stuffed in the brassiere she left only blobs of conscience congealing and congealing with his cries. One day he would come home and it would be like a corpse in the closet. Stuffed with two denials. Perhaps one a little bigger than the other. Or he would suddenly see it in a corner of the bedroom like a distant goggle, eyeless at his passion. One thing for sure. Somewhere it was waiting viciously to devour the small security he had. Till then, till that last supper it would make of him, daintily he danced on the razor.

2 Excerpt From The Divorce Proceedings

After the judge had examined all the tiny marks of countless keys, the lock of lips left undone at her mouth, the red welt about her neck where she had been his bouttoniere he asked: 'And is the other woman present in this courtroom?' 'Yes she is,' the wife replied, lifting up her finger to point. She had a truck tire for a wedding ring on that finger but still she pointed. She pointed at what appeared to be a huge piece of Swiss or Limburger cheese at the back of the courtroom.

'NO! NO!' cried out the 'monogamist', jangling a tiny foetal skeleton unconsciously in his pocket. 'She is just a razor. A razor. A razor. And you, judge, you are a razor, and my hands — they are both razors and they both cut at me, and every woman to every man and every night in every bed is a razor a razor a razor a razor . . .'

3 For Alimony She Got

One nostril anvil. Two avuncular aunts without morals or tongues. Three black and white zoot suits with armless and legless dependents in them. A team of interlocking dog's legs. A cheese player (stereo) and a yogurt recorder with matching cassettes. A mouse that wore knuckle-dusters made out of fetlock and sheep dip. A ship with *and* without an asshole. Something quite humourous. A lobotomized tomato, a month's subscription to *Lock and Bar*, and last but not least a manilla envelope full of circles that were not round. These last she put up on the wall pretending sometimes in her agony and solitude that they were holes winds whipped through when in the dark she seemed to feel a chill.

'Unless The Eye Catch Fire . . .'

P.K. Page

Unless the Eye catch fire
The God will not be seen . . .
Theodore Roszak

WEDNESDAY, SEPTEMBER 17.

The day began normally enough. The quails, cockaded as antique foot soldiers, arrived while I was having breakfast. The males black-faced, white-necklaced, cinnamon-crowned, with short, sharp dark plumes. Square bibs, Payne's grey; belly and sides with a pattern of small stitches. Reassuring, the flock of them. They tell me the macadamization of the world is not complete.

A sudden alarm, and as if they had one brain among them, they were gone in a rush — a sideways ascending Niagara — shutting out the light, obscuring the sky and exposing a rectangle of lawn, unexpectedly emerald. How bright the berries on the cotoneaster. Random leaves on the cherry twirled like gold spinners. The garden was high-keyed, vivid, locked in aspic.

Without warning, and as if I were looking down the tube of a kaleidoscope, the merest shake occurred — moiréed the garden — rectified itself. Or, more precisely, as if a range-finder through which I had been sighting, found of itself a more accurate focus. Sharpened, in fact, to an excoriating exactness.

And then the colours changed. Shifted to a higher octave — a *bright spectrum*. Each colour with its own *light*, its own *shape*. The leaves of the trees, the berries, the grasses — as if shedding successive films — disclosed layer after layer of hidden perfections. And upon these rapidly changing surfaces the 'range-finder' — to really play hob with metaphor! — sharpened its small invisible blades.

I don't know how to describe the intensity and speed of focus of this gratuitous zoom lens through which I stared, or the swift and dizzying adjustments within me. I became a 'sleeping top', perfectly centred, perfectly — sighted. The colours vibrated beyond the visible range of the spectrum. Yet I saw them. With some matching eye. Whole galaxies of them, blazing and glowing, flowing in rivulets, gushing in fountains — volatile, mercurial, and making lack-luster and off-key the colours of the rainbow.

I had no time or inclination to wonder, intellectualize. My mind seemed astonishingly clear and quite still. Like a crystal. A burning glass.

And then the range-finder sharpened once again. To alter space.

The lawn, the bushes, the trees — still super-brilliant — were no longer *there*. *There*, in fact, had ceased to exist. They were now, of all places in the world, *here*. Right in the centre of my being. Occupying an immense inner space. Part of me. Mine. Except the whole idea of ownership was beside the point. As true to say I was theirs as they mine. I and they were here; they and I, there. (*There, here* . . . odd . . . but for an irrelevant, inconsequential 't' which comes and goes, the words are the same.)

As suddenly as the world had altered, it returned to normal. I looked at my watch. A ridiculous mechanical habit. As I had no idea when the experience began it was impossible to know how long it had lasted. What had seemed eternity couldn't have been more than a minute or so. My coffee was still steaming in its mug.

The garden, through the window, was as it had always been. Yet not as it had always been. Less. Like listening to mono after hearing stereo. But with a far greater loss of dimension. A grievous loss.

I rubbed my eyes. Wondered, not without alarm, if this was the onset of some disease of the retina — glaucoma or some cellular change in the eye itself — superlatively packaged, fatally sweet as the marzipan cherry I ate as a child and *knew* was poison.

If it *is* a disease, the symptoms will recur. It will happen again.

TUESDAY, SEPTEMBER 23

It *has* happened again.

Tonight, taking Dexter for his late walk, I looked up at the crocheted tangle of boughs against the sky. Dark silhouettes against the lesser dark, but beating now with an extraordinary black brilliance. The golden glints in obsidian or the lurking embers in black opals are the nearest I can come to describing them. But it's a false description, emphasizing as it does, the wrong end of the scale. This was a *dark spectrum*. As if the starry heavens were translated into densities of black — black Mars, black Saturn, black Jupiter; or a master jeweller had crossed his jewels with jet and set them to burn and wink in the branches and twigs of oaks whose leaves shone luminous — a leafy Milky Way — fired by black chlorophyll.

Dexter stopped as dead as I. Transfixed. His thick honey-coloured coat and amber eyes glowing with their own intense brightness, suggested yet another spectrum. A *spectrum of light*. He was a constellated dog, shining, supra-real, against the foothills and mountain ranges of midnight.

I am reminded now, as I write, of a collection of lepidoptera in Brazil — one entire wall covered with butterflies, creatures of daylight — enormous or tiny — blue, orange, black. Strong-coloured. And on the opposite wall their anti-selves — pale night flyers spanning such a range of silver and white and lightest snuff-colour that once one entered their spectral scale there was no end to the subtleties and delicate nuances. But I didn't think like this then. All thought all comparisons were prevented by the startling infinities of darkness and light.

Then, as before, the additional shake occurred and the two spectrums moved swiftly from without to within. As if two equal and complementary circles centred inside me — or I in them. How explain that I not only *saw* but actually *was* the two spectrums? (I underline a simple, but in this case, exactly appropriate anagram.)

Then the range-finder lost its focus and the world, once again, was back to normal. Dexter, a pale, blurred blob, bounded about within the field of my peripheral vision, going on with his doggy interests just as if a moment before he had not been frozen in his tracks, a dog entranced.

I am no longer concerned about my eyesight. Wonder only if we are both mad. Dexter and I? Angelically mad, sharing hallucinations of epiphany. *Folie à deux?*

FRIDAY, OCTOBER 3.

It's hard to account for my secrecy, for I *have* been secretive. As if the cat had my tongue. It's not that I don't long to talk about the colours but I can't risk the wrong response — (as Gaby once said of a companion after a faultless performance of *Giselle*: 'If she had criticised the least detail of it, I'd have hit her!').

Once or twice I've gone so far as to say, 'I had the most extraordinary experience the other day . . .' hoping to find some look or phrase, some answering, 'So did I.' None has been forthcoming.

I can't forget the beauty. Can't get it out of my head. Startling, unearthly, indescribable. Infuriatingly indescribable. A glimpse of — somewhere else. Somewhere alive, miraculous, newly-made yet timeless. And more important still — significant, luminous, with a meaning of which I was part. Except that I — the I who is writing this — did not exist: was flooded out, dissolved in that immensity where subject and object are one.

I have to make a deliberate effort now not to live my life in terms of it; not to sit, immobilized, awaiting the shake that heralds a new world. Awaiting the transfiguration.

Luckily the necessities of life keep me busy. But upstream of my actions, behind a kind of plate glass, some part of me waits, listens, maintains a total attention.

TUESDAY, OCTOBER 7.

Things are moving very fast.

Some nights ago my eye was caught by a news item. 'Trucker Blames Colours', went the headline. Reading on: 'R. T. Ballantyne, driver for Island Trucks, failed to stop on a red light at the intersection of Fernhill and Spender. Questioned by traffic police, Ballantyne replied: "I didn't see it, that's all. There was this shake, then all these colours suddenly in the trees. Real bright ones I'd never seen before. I guess they must have blinded me." A breathalizer test proved negative. Full stop.'

I had an overpowering desire to talk to R. T. Ballantyne. Even looked him up in the telephone book. Not listed. I debated reaching him through Island Trucks in the morning.

Hoping for some mention of the story, I switched on the local radio station, caught the announcer mid-sentence: '. . . to come to the studio and talk to us. So far no one has been able to describe just what the "new" colours are, but perhaps Ruby Howard can. Ruby, you say you actually *saw* "new" colours?'

What might have been a flat, rather ordinary female voice was sharpened by wonder. 'I was out in the garden, putting it

126

to bed, you might say, getting it ready for winter. The hydrangeas are dried out — you know the way they go. Soft beiges and greys. And I was thinking maybe I should cut them back, when there was this — shake, like — and there they were shining. Pink. And blue. But not like they are in life. Different. Brighter. With little lights, like . . .'

The announcer's voice cut in, 'You say "not like they are in life". D'you think this wasn't life? I mean, do you think maybe you were dreaming?'

'Oh, no,' answered my good Mrs. Howard, positive, clear, totally unrattled. 'Oh, no, I wasn't *dreaming*. Not *dreaming* . . . Why — *this* is more like dreaming.' She was quiet a moment and then, in a matter-of-fact voice, 'I can't expect you to believe it,' she said. 'Why should you? I wouldn't believe it myself if I hadn't seen it.' Her voice expressed a kind of compassion as if she was really sorry for the announcer.

I picked up the telephone book for the second time, looked up the number of the station. I had decided to tell Mrs. Howard what I had seen. I dialled, got a busy signal, depressed the bar and waited, cradle in hand. I dialled again. And again.

LATER.

J. just phoned. Curious how she and I play the same game over and over.

J: Were you watching Channel 8?

Me: No, I . . .

J: An interview. With a lunatic. One who sees colours and flashing lights.

Me: Tell me about it.

J: He was a logger — a high-rigger — not that that has anything to do with it. He's retired now and lives in an apartment and has a window-box with geraniums. This morning the flowers were like neon, he said, flashing and shining . . . *Hon*estly!

Me: Perhaps he saw something you can't . . .

J: (*Amused*) I might have known you'd take his side. Seriously, what *could* he have seen?

Me: Flashing and shining — as he said.

J: But they couldn't. Not geraniums. And you know it as well as I do. *Hon*estly, Babe . . . (She is the only person left who calls me the name my mother called me.) Why are you always so perverse?

I felt faithless. I put down the receiver, as if I had not borne witness to my God.

Floods of letters to the papers. Endless interviews on radio and TV Pros, cons, inevitable spoofs.

One develops an eye for authenticity. It's as easy to spot as sunlight. However they may vary in detail, true accounts of the colour have an unmistakable common factor — a common factor as difficult to convey as sweetness to those who know only salt. True accounts are inarticulate, diffuse, unlikely — impossible.

It's recently crossed my mind that there may be some relationship between having seen the colours and their actual manifestation — something as improbable as *the more one sees them the more they are able to be seen*. Perhaps they are always there in some normally invisible part of the electro-magnetic spectrum and only become visible to certain people at certain times. A combination of circumstances or some subtle refinement in the organ of sight. And then — from quantity to quality perhaps, like water to ice — a whole community changes, is able to see, catches fire.

For example, it was seven days between the first time I saw the colours and the second. During that time there were no reports to the media. But once the reports began, the time between lessened appreciably *for me*. Not proof, of course, but worth noting. And I can't help wondering why some people see the colours and others don't. Do some of us have extra visision? Are some so conditioned that they're virtually blind to what's there before their very noses? Is it a question of more, or less?

Reports come in from farther and farther afield; from all walks of life. I think now there is no portion of the inhabited globe without 'shake freaks' and no acceptable reason for the sightings. Often only one member of a family will testify to the heightened vision. In my own small circle, I am the only witness — or so I think. I feel curiously hypocritical as I listen to my friends denouncing the 'shakers'. Drugs, they say. Irrational — possibly dangerous. Although no sinister incidents have occurred yet — just some mild shake-baiting here and there — one is uneasily reminded of Salem.

Scientists pronounce us hallucinated or mistaken, pointing

out that so far there is no hard evidence, no objective proof. That means, I suppose, no photographs, no spectroscopic measurement — if such is possible. Interestingly, seismographs show very minor earthquake tremors — showers of them, like shooting stars in August. Pundits claim 'shake fever' — as it has come to be called — is a variant on flying saucer fever and that it will subside in its own time. Beneficent physiologists suggest we are suffering (why is it *always* suffering, never enjoying?) a distorted form of *ocular spectrum* or after-image. (An after-image of what?) Psychologists disagree among themselves. All in all, it is not surprising that some of us prefer to keep our experiences to ourselves.

JANUARY 9.

Something new has occurred. Something impossible. Disturbing. So disturbing, in fact, that according to rumour it is already being taken with the utmost seriousness at the highest levels. TV, press and radio — with good reason — talk of little else.

What seemingly began as a mild winter has assumed sinister overtones. Farmers in southern Alberta are claiming the earth is unnaturally hot to the touch. Golfers at Harrison complain that the soles of their feet burn. Here on the coast, we notice it less. Benign winters are our specialty.

Already we don't lack for explanations as to why the earth could not be hotter than usual, nor why it is naturally 'unnaturally' hot. Vague notes of reassurance creep into the speeches of public men. They may be unable to explain the issue, but they can no longer ignore it.

To confuse matters further, reports on temperatures seem curiously inconsistent. What information we get comes mainly from self-appointed 'earth touchers'. And now that the least thing can fire an argument, their conflicting readings lead often enough to inflammatory debate.

For myself, I can detect no change at all in my own garden.

THURSDAY . . .?

There is no longer any doubt. The temperature of the earth's surface *is* increasing.

It is unnerving, horrible, to go out and feel the ground like some great beast, warm, beneath one's feet. As if another presence — vast, invisible — attends one. Dexter, too, is perplexed. He barks at the earth with the same indignation and, I suppose, fear, with which he barks at the first rumblings of earth-quake.

Air temperatures, curiously, don't increase proportionately — or so we're told. It doesn't make sense, but at the moment nothing makes sense. Countless explanations have been offered. Elaborate explanations. None adequate. The fact that the air temperature remains temperate despite the higher ground heat must, I think, be helping to keep panic down. Even so, these are times of great tension.

Hard to understand these two unexplained — unrelated? — phenomena: the first capable of dividing families; the second menacing us all. We are like animals trapped in a burning building.

LATER.

J. just phoned. Terrified. Why don't I move in with her, she urges. After all she has the space and we have known each other forty years. (Hard to believe when I don't feel even forty!) She can't bear it — the loneliness.

Poor J. Always so protected, insulated by her money. And her charm. What one didn't provide, the other did . . . diversions, services, attention.

What do I think is responsible for the heat, she asks. But it turns out she means who. Her personal theory is that the 'shake-freaks' are causing it — involuntarily, perhaps, but the two are surely linked.

'How could they possibly cause it?' I enquire. 'By what reach of the imagination . . .?'

'Search *me*!' she protests. 'How on earth should *I* know?' And the sound of the dated slang makes me really laugh.

But suddenly she is close to tears. 'How can you *laugh*?' she calls. 'This is nightmare. Nightmare!'

Dear J. I wish I could help but the only comfort I could offer would terrify her still more.

SEPTEMBER

Summer calmed us down. If the earth was hot, well, summers

are hot. And we were simply having an abnormally hot one.

Now that it is fall — the season of cool nights, light frosts — and the earth like a feverish child remains worryingly hot, won't cool down, apprehension mounts.

At last we are given official readings. For months the authorities have assured us with irrefutable logic that the temperature of the earth could not be increasing. Now, without any apparent period of indecision or confusion, they are warning us with equal conviction and accurate statistical documentation that it has, in fact, increased. Something anyone with a pocket-handkerchief of lawn has known for some time.

Weather stations, science faculties, astronomical observatories all over the world, are measuring and reporting. Intricate computerized tables are quoted. Special departments of government have been set up. We speak now of a new Triassic Age — the Neo-Triassic — and of the accelerated melting of the ice caps. But we are elaborately assured that this could not, repeat not, occur in our lifetime.

Interpreters and analysts flourish. The media are filled with theories and explanations. The increased temperature has been attributed to impersonal agencies such as bacteria from outer space; a thinning of the earth's atmosphere; a build-up of carbon-dioxide in the air; some axial irregularity; a change in the earth's core (geologists are reported to have begun test borings). No theory is too far-fetched to have its supporters. And because man likes a scapegoat, blame has been laid upon NASA, atomic physicists, politicians, the occupants of flying saucers and finally upon mankind at large — improvident, greedy mankind — whose polluted, strike-ridden world is endangered now by the fabled flames of hell.

We are also informed that Nostradamus, the Bible, and Jeane Dixon have all foreseen our plight. A new paperback, *Let Edgar Casey Tell You Why* sold out in a matter of days. Attendance at churches has doubled. Cults proliferate. Yet even in this atmosphere, we, the 'shake freaks', are considered lunatic fringe. Odd-men out. In certain quarters I believe we are seriously held responsible for the escalating heat, so J. is not alone. There have now been one or two nasty incidents. It is not surprising that even the most vocal among us have grown less willing to talk. I am glad to have kept silent. As a woman living alone, the less I draw attention to myself the better.

Our lives are greatly altered by this overhanging sense of doom. It is already hard to buy certain commodities. Dairy products are in very short supply. On the other hand, the market is flooded with citrus fruits. We are threatened with severe shortages for the future. The authorities are resisting rationing but it will have to come if only to prevent artificial shortages resulting from hoarding.

Luckily the colours are an almost daily event. I see them now, as it were, with my entire being. It is as if all my cells respond to their brilliance and become light too. At such times I feel I might shine in the dark.

NO IDEA OF THE DATE.

It is evening and I am tired but I am so far behind in my notes I want to get something down. Events have moved too fast for me.

Gardens, parks, every tillable inch of soil have been appropriated for food crops. As an able, if aging body, with an acre of land and some knowledge of gardening, I have been made responsible for soy-beans — small trifoliate plants rich with the promise of protein. Neat rows of them cover what were once my vegetable garden, flower beds, lawn.

Young men from the Department of Agriculture came last month, bull-dozed, cultivated, planted. Efficient, noisy desecrators of my twenty years of landscaping. Dexter barked at them from the moment they appeared and I admit I would have shared his indignation had the water shortage not already created its own desolation.

As a government gardener I'm a member of a new privileged class. I have watering and driving permits and coupons for gasoline and boots — an indication of what is to come. So far there has been no clothes rationing.

Daily instructions — when to water and how much, details of mulching, spraying — reach me from the government radio station to which I tune first thing in the morning. It also provides temperature readings, weather forecasts and the latest news releases on emergency measures, curfews, rationing, insulation. From the way things are going I think it will soon be our only station. I doubt that newspapers will be able to print much longer. In any event, I have already given them up. At first it was interesting to see how quickly drugs, pollution, education, Women's Lib., all became by-gone issues; and, initially, I was

132

fascinated to see how we rationalized. Then I became bored. Then disheartened. Now I am too busy.

EVENING.

A call came from J. Will I come for Christmas?

Christmas! Extraordinary thought. Like a word from another language learned in my youth, now forgotten.

'I've still got some Heidseck. We can get tight.'

The word takes me back to my teens. 'Like old times . . .'

'Yes.' She is eager. I hate to let her down. 'J., I can't. How could I get to you?'

'In your *car*, silly. *You* still have gas. You're the only one of us who has.' Do I detect a slight hint of accusation, as if I had acquired it illegally?

'But J., it's only for emergencies.'

'My God, Babe, d'you think *this* isn't an emergency?'

'J., dear . . .'

'*Please*, Babe,' she pleads: 'I'm so afraid. Of the looters. The eeriness. You must be afraid too, *Please!*'

I should have said, yes, that of course I was afraid. It's only natural to be afraid. Or, unable to say that, I should have made the soothing noises a mother makes to her child. Instead, 'There's no reason to be afraid, J.,' I said. It must have sounded insufferably pompous.

'No reason!' She was exasperated with me. 'I'd have thought there was every reason.'

She will phone again. In the night perhaps when she can't sleep. Poor J. She feels so alone. She *is* so alone. And so idle. I don't suppose it's occurred to her yet that telephones will soon go. That a whole way of life is vanishing completely.

It's different for me. I have the soy-beans which keep me busy all the daylight hours. And Dexter. And above all I have the colours and with them the knowledge that there are others, other people, whose sensibilities I share. We are invisibly, inviolably related to one another as the components of a molecule. I say 'we'. Perhaps I should speak only for myself, yet I feel as sure of these others as if they had spoken. Like the quails, we share one brain — no, I think it is one heart — between us. How do I know this? How *do* I know? I know by knowing. We are less alarmed by the increasing heat than those

133

who have not seen the colours. I can't explain why. But seeing the colours seems to change one — just as certain diagnostic procedures cure the complaint they are attempting to diagnose.

In all honesty I admit to having had moments when this sense of community was not enough, when I have had a great longing for my own kind — for so have I come to think of these others — in the way one has a great longing for someone one loves. Their presence in the world is not enough. One must see them. Touch them. Speak with them.

But lately that longing has lessened. All longing, in fact. And fear. Even my once great dread that I might cease to see the colours has vanished. It is as if through seeing them I have learned to see them. Have learned to be ready to see — passive; not striving to see — active. It keeps me very wide awake. Transparent even. Still.

The colours come daily now. Dizzying. Tranforming. Lifegiving. My sometimes back-breaking toil in the garden is lightened, made full of wonder, by the incredible colours shooting in the manner of children's sparklers from the plants themselves and from my own work-worn hands. I hadn't realized that I too am part of this vibrating luminescence.

LATER.

I have no idea how long it is since I abandoned these notes. Without seasons to measure its passing, without normal activities — preparations for festivals, occasional outings — time feels longer, shorter or — more curious still — simultaneous, undifferentiated. Future and past fused in the present. Linearity broken.

I had intended to write regularly, but the soy-beans keep me busy pretty well all day and by evening I'm usually ready for bed. I'm sorry however to have missed recording the day-by-day changes. They were more or less minor at first. But once the heat began its deadly escalation, the world as we have known it — 'our world' — had you been able to put it alongside 'this world' — would have seemed almost entirely different.

No one, I think, could have foreseen the speed with which everything has broken down. For instance, the elaborate plans made to maintain transportation became useless in a matter of months. Private traffic was first curtailed, then forbidden. If a man from another planet had looked in on us, he would have been astonished to see us trapped who were apparently free.

The big changes only really began after the first panic evacuations from the cities. Insulated by concrete, sewer pipes and underground parkades, high density areas responded slowly to the increasing temperatures. But once the heat penetrated their insulations, Gehennas were created overnight and whole populations fled in hysterical exodus, jamming highways in their futile attempts to escape.

Prior to this the government had not publicly acknowledged a crisis situation. They had taken certain precautions, brought in temporary measures to ease shortages and dealt with new developments on an *ad hoc* basis. Endeavoured to play it cool. Or so it seemed. Now they levelled with us. It was obvious that they must have been planning for months, only awaiting the right psychological moment to take everything over. That moment had clearly come. What we had previously thought of as a free world ended. We could no longer eat, drink, move without permits or coupons. This was full-scale emergency.

Yet nothing proceeds logically. Plans are made only to be remade to accommodate new and totally unexpected developments. The heat, unpatterened as disseminated sclerosis, attacks first here, then there. Areas of high temperature suddenly and inexplicably cool off — or vice versa. Agronomists are doing everything possible to keep crops coming — taking advantage of hot-house conditions to force two crops where one had grown before — frantically playing a kind of agricultural roulette, gambling on the length of time a specific region might continue to grow temperate-zone produce.

Mails have long since stopped. And newspapers. And telephones. As a member of a new privileged class, I have been equipped with a two way radio and a permit to drive on government business. Schools have of course closed. An attempt was made for a time to provide lessons over tv. Thankfully the looting and rioting seem over. Those desperate gangs of angry citizens who for some time made life additionally difficult, have now disappeared. We seem at last to understand that we are all in this together.

Life is very simple without electricity. I get up with the light and go to bed as darkness falls. My food supply is still substantial and because of the soy-bean crop I am all right for water. Dexter has adapted well to his new life. He is outdoors less than he used to be and has switched to a mainly vegetable diet without too much difficulty.

This morning a new order over the radio. All of us with special driving privileges were asked to report to our zone garage to have our tires treated with heat resistant plastic.

I had not been into town for months. I felt rather as one does on returning home from hospital — that the world is unexpectedly large, with voluminous airy spaces. This was exaggerated perhaps by the fact that our whole zone had been given over to soy-beans. Everywhere the same rows of green plants — small pods already formed — march across gardens and boulevards. I was glad to see the climate prove so favourable. But there was little else to make me rejoice as I drove through ominously deserted streets, paint blistering and peeling on fences and houses, while overhead a haze of dust, now always with us, created a green sun.

The prolonged heat has made bleak the little park opposite the garage. A rocky little park, once all mosses and rhododendrons, it is bare now, and brown. I was seeing the day as everyone saw it. Untransmuted.

As I stepped out of my car to speak to the attendant I cursed that I had not brought my insulators. The burning tarmac made me shift rapidly from foot to foot. Anyone from another planet would have wondered at this extraordinary quirk of earthlings. But my feet were forgotten as my eyes alighted a second time on the park across the way. I had never before seen so dazzling and variegated a display of colours. How could there be such prismed brilliance in the range of greys and browns? It was as if the perceiving organ — wherever it is — sensitized by earlier experience, was now correctly tuned for this further perception.

The process was as before: the merest shake and the whole park was 'rainbow, rainbow, rainbow'. A further shake brought the park from *there* to *here*. Interior. But this time the interior space had increased. Doubled. By a kind of instant knowledge that rid me of all doubt, I knew that the garage attendant was seeing it too. *We saw the colours.*

Then, with that slight shift of focus, as if a gelatinous film had moved briefly across my sight, everything slipped back.

I really looked at the attendant for the first time. He was a skinny young man standing up naked inside a pair of loose striped overalls cut off at the knee, *sidney* embroidered in red over his left breast pocket. He was blonde, small-boned, with nothing about him to stick in the memory except his clear eyes which at that moment bore an expression of total comprehension.

'You . . .' we began together and laughed.

'Have you seen them before?' I asked. But it was rather as one would say 'how do you do' — not so much a question as a salutation.

We looked at each other for a long time, as if committing each other to memory.

'Do you know anyone else?' I said.

'One or two. Three, actually. Do you?'

I shook my head. 'You are the first. Is it . . . is it . . . always like that?'

'You mean . . .?' he gestured towards his heart.

I nodded.

'Yes,' he said. 'Yes, it is.'

There didn't seem anything more to talk about. Your right hand hasn't much to say to your left, or one eye to the other. There was comfort in the experience, if comfort is the word, which it isn't. More as if an old faculty had been extended. Or a new one activated.

Sidney put my car on the hoist and sprayed its tires.

SOME TIME LATER.

I have not seen Sidney again. Two weeks ago when I went back he was not there and as of yesterday, cars have become obsolete. Not that we will use that word publicly. The official word is *suspended*.

Strange to be idle after months of hard labor. A lull only before the boys from the Department of Agriculture come back to prepare the land again. I am pleased that the soy-beans are harvested, that I was able to nurse them along to maturity despite the scorching sun, the intermittent plagues and the problems with water. Often the pressure was too low to turn the sprinklers and I would stand, hour after hour, hose in hand, trying to get the most use from the tiny trickle spilling from the nozzle.

Sometimes my heart turns over as I look through the kitchen window and see the plants shrivelled and grotesque, the baked earth scored by a web of fine cracks like the glaze on a plate subjected to too high an oven. Then it comes to me in a flash that of course, the beans are gone, the harvest is over.

The world is uncannily quiet. I don't think anyone had any idea of how much noise even distant traffic made until we were without it. It is rare indeed for vehicles other than Government mini-cars to be seen on the streets. And there are fewer and fewer pedestrians. Those who do venture out, move on their thick insulators with the slow gait of rocking-horses. Surreal and alien, they heighten rather than lessen one's sense of isolation. For one *is* isolated. We have grown used to the sight of helicopters like large dragon-flies hovering overhead — addressing us through their P.A. systems, dropping supplies — welcome but impersonal.

Dexter is my only physical contact. He is delighted to have me inside again. The heat is too great for him in the garden and as, officially, he no longer exists, we only go out under cover of dark.

The order to destroy pets, when it came, indicated more clearly than anything that had gone before, that the government had abandoned hope. In an animal-loving culture, only direct necessity could validate such an order. It fell upon us like a heavy pall.

When the Government truck stopped by for Dexter, I reported him dead. Now that the welfare of so many depends upon our cooperation with authority, law-breaking is a serious offence. But I am not uneasy about breaking this law. As long as he remains healthy and happy, Dexter and I will share our dwindling provisions.

No need to be an ecologist or dependent on non-existant media to know all life is dying and the very atmosphere of our planet is changing radically. Already no birds sing in the hideous hot dawns as the sun, rising through a haze of dust, sheds its curious bronze-green light on a brown world. The trees that once gave us shade stand leafless now in an infernal winter. Yet, as if in the masts and riggings of ships, St. Elmo's fire flickers and shines in their high branches, and bioplasmic pyrotechnics light the dying soy-beans. I am reminded of how the ghostly form of a limb remains attached to the body from which it has been amputated. And I can't help thinking of all the people who don't see the colours, the practical earth-touchers with only their blunt senses to inform them. I wonder about J. and if, since we last talked, she has perhaps been able to see the colours too. But I think not. After so many years of friendship, surely I would be able to sense her, had she broken through.

The heat has increased greatly in the last few weeks — in a quantum leap. This has resulted immediately in two things: a steady rising of the sea level throughout the world — with panic reactions and mild flooding in coastal areas; and, at last, a noticeably higher air temperature. It is causing great physical discomfort.

It was against this probability that the authorities provided us with insulator spray. Like giant cans of pressurized shaving cream. I have shut all rooms but the kitchen and by concentrating my insulating zeal on this one small area, we have managed to keep fairly cool. The word is relative, of course. The radio has stopped giving temperature readings and I have no thermometer. I have filled all cracks and crannies with the foaming plastic, even applied a layer to the exterior wall. There are no baths, of course, and no cold drinks. On the other hand I've abandoned clothes and given Dexter a shave and a haircut. Myself as well. We are a fine pair. Hairless and naked.

When the world state of emergency was declared we didn't need to be told that science had given up. The official line had been that the process would reverse itself as inexplicably as it had begun. The official policy — to hold out as long as possible. With this in mind task forces worked day and night on survival strategy. On the municipal level, which is all I really knew about, everything that could be centralized was. Telephone exchanges, hydro plants, radio stations became centres around which vital activities took place. Research teams investigated the effects of heat on water mains, sewer pipes, electrical wiring; work crews were employed to prevent, protect or even destroy incipient causes of fire, flood and asphyxiation.

For some time now the city has been zoned. In each zone a large building has been selected, stocked with food, medical supplies and insulating materials. We have been provided with zone maps and an instruction sheet telling us to stay where we are until ordered to move to what is euphemistically called our 'home'. When ordered, we are to load our cars with whatever we still have of provisions and medicines and drive off *at once*. Helicopters have already dropped kits with enough gasoline for the trip and a small packet, somewhat surprisingly labelled 'emergency rations' which contains one cyanide capsule — grim reminder that all may not go as the planners plan. We have been asked to mark our maps, in advance, with the shortest route from our house to our 'home', so that in a crisis we will know what we are doing. These instructions are repeated *ad nauseam* over the radio, along with hearty assurances that everything is under control and that there is no cause for alarm. The Government station is now all that remains of our multi-media. When it is not broadcasting instructions, its mainly pre-recorded tapes sound inanely complacent and repetitive. Evacuation Day, as we have been told again and again, will be announced by whistle blast. Anyone who runs out of food before that or who is in need of medical aid is to use the special gas ration and go 'home' at once.

As a long-time preserver of fruits and vegetables, I hope to hold out until E. Day. When that time comes it will be a sign that broadcasts are no longer possible, that contact can no longer be maintained between the various areas of the community, that the process will not reverse itself in time and that, in fact, our world is well on the way to becoming — oh, wonder of the modern kitchen — a self-cleaning oven.

SPRING, SUMMER, WINTER, FALL.
WHAT SEASON IS IT AFTER ALL?

I sense the hours by some inner clock. I have applied so many layers of insulating spray that almost no heat comes through from outside. But we have to have air and the small window I have left exposed acts like a furnace. Yet through it I see the dazzling colours; sense my fellow-men.

NOON.

The sun is hidden directly overhead. The world is topaz. I see it through the minute eye of my window. I, the perceiving organ that that peers through the house's only aperture. We are one, the house and I — parts of some vibrating sensitive organism in which Dexter plays his differentiated but integral role. The light enters us, dissolves us. We are the golden motes in the jewel.

MIDNIGHT.

The sun is directly below. Beneath the burning soles of my arching feet it shines, a globe on fire. Its rays penetrate the earth. Upward beaming, they support and sustain us. We are held aloft, a perfectly balanced ball in the jet of a golden fountain. Light, dancing, infinitely upheld.

WHO KNOWS HOW MUCH LATER.

I have just 'buried' Dexter.

This morning I realized this hot little cell was no longer a possible place for a dog.

I had saved one can of dog food against this day. As I opened it Dexter's eyes swivelled in the direction of so unexpected and delicious a smell. He struggled to his feet, joyous, animated. The old Dexter. I was almost persuaded to delay, to wait and see if the heat subsided. What if tomorrow we awakened to rain? But something in me, stronger than this wavering self, carried on with its purpose.

He sat up, begging, expectant.

I slipped the meat out of the can.

'You're going to have a really good dinner,' I said, but as my voice was unsteady, I stopped.

I scooped a generous portion of the meat into his dish and placed it on the floor. He was excited, and as always when excited about food, he was curiously ceremonial, unhurried — approaching his dish and backing away from it, only to approach it again at a slightly different angle. As if the exact position was of the greatest importance. It was one of his most amusing and endearing characteristics. I let him eat his meal in his own leisurely and appreciative manner and then, as I have done so many times before, I fed him his final *bon bouche* by hand. The cyanide pill, provided by a beneficent government for me, went down in a gulp.

I hadn't expected it to be so sudden. Life and death so close. His small frame convulsed violently, then collapsed. Simultaneously, as if synchronized, the familiar 'shake' occurred in my vision. Dexter glowed brightly, whitely, like phosphorus. In that dazzling, light-filled moment he was no longer a small dead dog lying there. I could have thought him a lion, my sense of scale had so altered. His beautiful body blinded me with its fires.

With the second 'shake' his consciousness must have entered mine for I felt a surge in my heart as if his loyalty and love had flooded it. And like a kind of ground bass, I was aware of scents

141

and sounds I had not known before. Then a great peace filled me — an immense space, light and sweet — and I realized that this was death. Dexter's death.

But how describe what is beyond description?

As the fires emanating from his slight frame died down, glowed weakly, residually, I put on my insulators and carried his body into the now fever-hot garden. I laid him on what had been at one time an azalea bed. I was unable to dig a grave in the baked earth or to cover him with leaves. But there are no predators now to pick the flesh from his bones. Only the heat which will, in time, desiccate it.

I returned to the house, opening the door as little as possible to prevent the barbs and briars of burning air from entering with me. I sealed the door from inside with foam sealer.

The smell of the canned dog food permeated the kitchen. It rang in my nostrils. Olfactory chimes, lingering, delicious. I was intensely aware of Dexter. Dexter imminent. I contained him as simply as a dish contains water. But the simile is not exact. For I missed his physical presence. One relies on the physical more than I had known. My hands sought palpable contact. The flesh forgets slowly.

Idly, abstractedly, I turned on the radio. I seldom do now as the batteries are low and they are my last. Also, there is little incentive. Broadcasts are intermittent and I've heard the old tapes over and over.

But the government station was on the air. I tuned with extreme care and placed my ear close to the speaker. A voice, faint, broken by static, sounded like that of the Prime Minster.

'. . . all human beings can do, your government has done for you.' (Surely not a political speech *now*?) 'But we have failed. Failed to hold back the heat. Failed to protect ourselves against it; to protect you against it. It is with profound grief that I send this farewell message to you all.' I realized that this, too, had been pre-recorded, reserved for the final broadcast. 'Even now, let us not give up hope . . .'

And then, blasting through the speech, monstrously loud in the stone-silent world, the screech of the whistle summoning us 'home'. I could no longer hear the P.M.'s words.

I began automatically, obediently, to collect my few remaining foodstuffs, reaching for a can of raspberries, the last of the crop to have grown in my garden when the dawns were dewy and cool and noon sun fell upon us like golden pollen. My hand stopped in mid-air.

I would not go 'home'.

The whistle shrilled for a very long time. A curious great steam-driven cry — man's last. Weird that our final utterance should be this anguished inhuman wail.

THE END.

Now that it is virtually too late, I regret not having kept a daily record. Now that the part of me that writes has become nearly absorbed, I feel obliged to do the best I can.

I am down to the last of my food and water. Have lived on little for some days — weeks, perhaps. How can one measure passing time? Eternal time grows like a tree, its roots in my heart. If I lie on my back I see winds moving in its high branches and a chorus of birds is singing in its leaves. The song is sweeter than any music I have ever heard.

My kitchen is as strange as I am myself. Its walls bulge with many layers of spray. It is without geometry. Like the inside of an eccentric styrofoam coconut. Yet, with some inner eye, I see its intricate mathematical structure. It is as ordered and no more random than an atom.

My face is unrecognizable in the mirror. Wisps of short damp hair. Enormous eyes. I swim in their irises. Could I drown in the pits of their pupils?

Through my tiny window when I raise the blind, a dead world shines. Sometimes dust storms fill the air with myriad particles burning bright and white as the lion body of Dexter. Sometimes great clouds swirl, like those from which saints receive revelations.

The colours are almost constant now. There are times when, light-headed, I dance a dizzying dance, feel part of that whirling incandescent matter — what I might once have called inorganic matter!

On still days the blameless air, bright as a glistening wing, hangs over us, hangs its extraordinary beneficence over us.

We are together now, united, indissoluble. Bonded.

Because there is no expectation, there is no frustration.

Because there is nothing we can have, there is nothing we can want.

We are hungry of course. Have cramps and weakness. But they are as if in *another body*. Our body is inviolate. Inviolable.

We share one heart.

143

We are one with the starry heavens and our bodies are stars.
Inner and outer are the same. A continuum. The water in the locks is level. We move to a higher water. A high sea.
A ship could pass through.

Contributors' Notes

GEORGE BOWERING (1935-) Born in Pentiction, he now lives in Vancouver and teaches at Simon Fraser University. Author of some two dozen books of poetry and fiction, he was awarded the Governor-General's Award for poetry in 1969 and for fiction in 1981. His books include *A Short Sad Book* and *Burning Water*.

CLAUDETTE CHARBONNEAU-TISSOT (1947-) Born in Montreal, she received her MA in French Literature from the University of Laval in 1974. For the past decade she has lived in Quebec City, where she now teaches at a community college. Her works include two collections of stories, *Contes pour hydrocéphales adultes* (1974) and *La contrainte* (1976), and a novel *La Chaise au fond de l'oeil* (1979), all published by Le Cercle du livre de France.

GEOFF HANCOCK (1946-) Born in New Westminster, B.C., he is editor-in-chief of *Canadian Fiction Magazine* and a freelance radio and magazine literary journalist. He has travelled widely in Asia, South America and Europe. His anthologies include *Magic Realism*, and with Rikki, the forthcoming *Shoes and Shit: stories for fetishists*.

W. P. KINSELLA (1935-) Born in Edmonton, he teaches fiction writing at the University of Calgary. His stories have appeared in numerous literary magazines as well as the collections of *Dance Me Outside, Scars* and *Shoeless Joe Jackson Comes to Iowa*. His novel, *Shoeless Joe*, won a Houghton-Mifflin Fellowship.

GARRY MCKEVITT (1947-) Born in Calgary, he received his BA in Creative Writing at the University of Victoria in 1979 and was awarded the Rosalind Hulet Petch Memorial Prize in Creative Writing at Victoria. Now directing and producing television programmes in Victoria, he has published poems and stories in various journals and broadsheets and is presently working on a collection of short stories.

EUGENE MCNAMARA (1930-) Born in Oak Park, Illinois. Married, he is now a Canadian citizen, teaching English at the University of Windsor and editing the University of Windsor Review. His work has appeared in many leading literary magazines and anthologies.

GEORGE MCWHIRTER (1939-) Born in Belfast, subsequently taught English there and at the University of Barcelona. Now teaching in the creative writing department at UBC. His first book *Catalan Poems* won the Commonwealth Poetry Prize. Other books include a book length poem *Queen of the Sea*, several chapbooks and broadsides, *The Island Man*, as well as stories collected in *Bodyworks, God's Eye*, and *Coming To Grips With Lucy*.

P. K. PAGE (1916-) Born in England and came to Canada in 1919. Her poems, stories, articles and graphics have appeared in Canada's leading literary and art magazines. Publications include *Cry Ararat, The Sun and the Moon and other fictions, Poems Selected and New*, and *To Say the Least* (ed.).

ROBERT PRIEST (1952-) Born in England, he is author of *The Visible Man* (Monument Press), *Sadness of Spacemen* (Dreadnaught) and *God or Opium?* (Dreadnaught). He is also a rock musician, singer and lyricist.

JAMES ROSS (1943-) Lives in Hamilton, Ontario and is Editor-in-Chief of a series of high school anthologies on CBC *Ideas* and his stories have appeared in *Prism, Canadian Forum, Dialogue* and CFM.

DERK WYNAND (1944-) Born in Bad Suderode, Germany, he emigrated to Canada in 1952 and attended UBC. He has published three collections of poems, *Locus, Snowscapes*, and *Pointwise* as well as the prose work *One Cook, Once Dreaming*. He currently teaches creative writing at the University of Victoria.